# Saving Grace

## Broken Fate, book two
### A Barrett's Bay Romance

## Emily Stormbrook

## Titles by Emily Stormbrook

**Addicted to Sin series:**
Breaking Sin
Mastering Sin
Marrying Sin (2022)

**Elswyth Chase series:**
Hel to Pay
Chasing Starlight
Frozen Hearts
Tainted Love
Soul's Gambit
Fierce Cravings
Savage blood
Spirit's salvation
Hidden Desires

**Barrett's Bay Romances:**

**Broken Fate:**
Tempting Fate
Saving Grace

Text Copyright © Emily Stormbrook
All rights reserved

First Edition
Version 1.0

This book is copyright. Subject to statutory exception and to provisions of relevant collective licensing agreements, no part of this publication may be reproduced, stored in a retrieval system, or transmitted in any form or by any means, without the prior written permission of the author.

This book is sold subject to the conditions that it shall not, by way of trade or otherwise, be lent, re-sold, hired out, or otherwise circulated without the publisher's prior consent in any form of binding or cover other than that which it is published and without a similar condition including this condition being imposed on the subsequent purchaser.

In this work of fiction, the characters, places and events are either the product of the author's imagination or they are used entirely fictitiously. Any resemblance to actual persons, living or dead, is purely coincidental.

| | |
|---|---|
| CHAPTER ONE | 1 |
| CHAPTER TWO | 24 |
| CHAPTER THREE | 39 |
| CHAPTER FOUR | 57 |
| CHAPTER FIVE | 66 |
| CHAPTER SIX | 84 |
| CHAPTER SEVEN | 99 |
| CHAPTER EIGHT | 111 |
| CHAPTER NINE | 128 |
| CHAPTER TEN | 161 |
| CHAPTER ELEVEN | 177 |
| CHAPTER TWELVE | 193 |
| CHAPTER THIRTEEN | 215 |
| CHAPTER FOURTEEN | 238 |
| CHAPTER FIFTEEN | 250 |
| CHAPTER SIXTEEN | 261 |
| CHAPTER SEVENTEEN | 274 |
| CHAPTER EIGHTEEN | 284 |
| CHAPTER NINETEEN | 304 |
| CHAPTER TWENTY | 312 |

There's a group of ladies who will likely never see this, but they were there for me when I felt alone and at my lowest.

This book is dedicated to them.

To Jessica, Andie, Lindsey, Pamela, and Lindsay-Jane.

Thank you x

## CHAPTER ONE

### Jesse

What had I done? I can still hear my voice, laced with venom and hatred as I looked at the woman I loved and tried to rip her apart. I should try to defend my actions, but there is no defence, no justification.

I'd been a dick. I hadn't let her talk or given her a chance to explain. I just took all her fears and insecurities, and turned them back on her, told her they were true.

I told her she'd never be enough for

anyone, when in fact, she was everything to me. Every-Goddamn-thing.

That was why, when I thought she'd betrayed me, it had destroyed me. In turn, I wanted to destroy her, make her feel the pain I was feeling. I should have taken a breath, should have paused to think. Because if I had, then I would have seen the danger.

When I found that blacked out marriage certificate on my desk, all I saw was red. I was back in the past, reliving the betrayal that broke me, the lies that made me never want to love again.

For almost three years I'd had an insatiable rage burning deep inside me. It never quietened, never dulled. It was always there, just under the surface, held in place by the force of my will.

Three years ago, I had come home to find my pregnant wife in bed with my best friend.

I'd done everything for that woman. I'd moved cities, transferred from my position in the NCA to the local PD, all so we could be closer to her family. I'd left almost every friend I'd ever made behind, all in the name of her happiness. There hadn't been a thing I wouldn't have done for her. Nothing I wouldn't have given her, which was just as well since she took everything.

When she told me she was pregnant it had come as a shock. Of course it had, we'd always been careful. Neither of us were ready for children. I had my career, and she ... well she was used to a certain lifestyle that I was expected to maintain.

I supported her when she quit her job just after we married. She wanted to pursue her dream of being a social media influencer, and my only wish had been to make her happy. She wore the hottest fashions, had the latest tech, and I worked every hour God sent to provide for her, to keep her in those tiny strips of branded panties that I never saw because I was rarely home.

Well, someone else had been enjoying them at my expense.

When I found out about the baby she'd already burned through my savings. I took a second job. There was no way my family would want for anything. I thought I loved her. Even when I realised we didn't even seem to like each other anymore, I still did everything I could to keep her happy. She was my wife. Looking after her was my responsibility.

Or it had been.

Right up until I found her in bed with Dale. It was the betrayal that cut the deepest, the secrets and lies that ate away at me. I had worked myself to death for her, and she had the nerve to complain I was never home. That was her excuse for sleeping with my best friend. The salt in the wounds had been when I later discovered the real reason she'd wanted to move, was not because she wanted her and the baby to be closer to her parents, it was to be closer to Dale.

The day I walked in to see her riding him like she was the star of a rodeo, that was it. I'd walked out the door, filed for divorce, and hadn't laid eyes on her since.

That was the day the quiet rage began to build. But I let it fester. It ate away at me from the inside out, made me question every relationship I'd ever built. If my wife and best friend could so easily betray me, then why should I trust anyone else?

My brother, Rob, had been my rock. He'd been the one to deal with her, acting as a go-between, ferrying papers back and forth between us while working in Barrett's Bay as their junior doctor and making sure I didn't drink too much.

He'd had his work cut out for him. When I held a beer in my hand, I'd known what to expect from it. I would drink, get drunk, and wake up feeling like shit. With a beer, I knew what I was getting into. People, however, didn't come with warning labels.

Through the entire divorce proceedings she'd led me along, letting me think the baby was mine, knowing I'd want to support my son in any way that I could. I gave her the car, what little savings I had scraped back together, I'd even said she could stay in my house rent-free until such a time I wanted it for myself. I gave her everything, and it turned out the damn kid wasn't even mine.

She'd used the baby as a pawn in her game. Even had the audacity to put my name on the birth certificate since our divorce hadn't been finalised. The moment I saw his picture I'd known he wasn't mine. Continuing the facade would have been like a tiger trying to convince the world it had given birth to an ostrich.

The boy looked just like his father, right down to his mocha skin and deep brown eyes. I hadn't needed to pay for a paternity test, but I had done so all the same. She had already taken me for almost everything I had. I'd be damned if I was paying child support for another man's child while they got to play happy family at my expense.

I'd rented a bedsit and stayed in my job at the PD, but I hadn't been happy. I missed my role in the NCA, but my pride wouldn't let me go crawling back with my hat in my hand and tail between my legs, begging for my old job back. I'd already failed as a husband and a man. I didn't want to be seen failing at my career too.

A few months ago, when Rob told me

that Major Donnelly was retiring and looking for a replacement back home, I'd jumped at the chance to return to Barrett's Bay. I hated the city, hated everything it stood for, and the reminders of betrayal I had to see on a daily basis. I was hurting, alone, and I couldn't even bring myself to trust my partner on the force, because all I could see was the potential of being betrayed again.

A cop needed to be able to trust their partner, not second guess their motive every time they made a suggestion.

I closed myself off, promising I'd never make the same mistake again, that I'd never trust anyone with my heart. And I'd been doing fine, right until I saw Miranda Grace standing in her grandparents' hall. It was in that moment, as my heart fluttered in my chest at the sight of her, and I began grinning like a loon, that I realised I had never really loved Abigail.

After Abigail and Dale had married, I had been waiting for the calls to start. She didn't have the nerve to see me in person, not that I would entertain the idea, but on the phone, she was always the same infuriating, entitled woman I recalled. I don't know what I ever saw in her. She only ever called when she wanted something, and since my name was still on her son's birth certificate, if Dale wanted parental rights, he had to adopt him, which meant I had to sign my rights away. The thought was a joke, how could I have parental rights for a child who so obviously wasn't mine?

The first time I'd kissed Grace had been on the back of that phone call. The woman had been impossible, demanding I got the forms back to her that day. It had been a Sunday, it wouldn't have made the blindest bit of difference, but she just kept pushing and pushing. She wouldn't let up and if there was one thing Abigail could do, it was push my buttons.

Speaking to her always put me on edge. That ball of rage inside me had calmed after seeing Grace. She had been the balm to soothe the burn. But each time my brother made her laugh, or shared a moment with her, it simmered again. Even as children I'd always seen Grace as mine.

# SAVING GRACE

Mine to protect. Mine to defend. Mine to hold. Mine to love. And how I had wanted to love her.

When puberty struck, things became a little awkward. Grace had always been one of the boys, scaling the cliffs, fishing in the rock pools, liberating crabs—all the while putting on a brave face because crabs were the spiders of the sea imbued with armour and weaponry, and if we knew one thing, it was that Grace was terrified of spiders. Even the tiniest money spider, dangled on a web, was enough to send her running.

By the time I turned sixteen I knew that, although I only saw her when schools were off, I didn't want to wait another moment to make her mine.

It was unbelievable. At school, I had girls throwing themselves at me. My brown hair and blue eyes seemed to draw them in. I only needed to wink to send my fan club into a giggling frenzy. They'd follow me around the school like lost puppies, reciting poems about how my eyes were like a summer sky. Grace always called them ocean blue. I liked that; it gave a sense of danger stirring beneath the surface. If she'd known the thoughts I had about her, how I'd wanted to sweep her away, she'd have realised why ocean blue was not as serene as she believed. But any time I tried to put a move on Grace, I froze.

Rob called her my summer love, although she visited every school holiday to get away from those awful parents of hers. She didn't speak much about them, but I knew there was something wrong at home. Whenever she arrived, she looked broken, tired, but being here breathed life into her. I loved watching that weight lift from her shoulders as she came alive.

It was just before her sixteenth birthday when I'd finally worked up the courage to kiss her. I'd had my fair share of kisses. I was practised, good even. I imagined how it would feel to slide my palm across her soft skin to cradle her face, teasing her plump lip with my thumb before pressing my lips to hers and sharing her breath. But when I leaned in, as the three of us watched fireworks, I panicked at the thought of

# SAVING GRACE

actually kissing the girl whose face I'd always imagined when kissing another. I chickened out, making some excuse for why I'd had leaned in so close. I don't even remember what it was, only that I cursed myself for years over the missed chance.

If I'd kissed her that day, maybe things would have somehow turned out differently.

I hadn't known that would be my last chance, hadn't imagined that a few days later my Grace would be torn away from me and I wouldn't see her again for years. Her gran received a phone call saying she had to go home. Weeks later, I remember them doing everything they could to try to get custody of their granddaughter, but no one would say why. Eventually, after years of trying, they were forced to give up.

She never came back.
Never visited.
Never wrote.

For eleven years she vanished without a trace, until she turned up here claiming to be Andy. At first, I thought she'd just shortened her first name, Miranda. But it soon became obvious she was hiding something, and that's when all this started. When my past sabotaged my chance of a future.

I never should have run that background check on her.

I'd regretted it the moment I'd done it.

Being a small town, I didn't have access to all the systems from the converted cottage we used as a precinct. I'd sent the request for the information to the main PD in the city. When the email came back, I was already riddled with guilt. The woman had walked back into my life after eleven years; I owed her the chance to tell me about her life without cheating, without using my position to uncover her secrets.

I never opened the email.

I was regretting that decision now.

Everything I'd never said to Abigail. The hurt, the anger, the betrayal, had all come flying out, but instead of being directed at the woman who deserved it, I fired my hatred at Grace.

Minimum effort. Maximum pain.

Even if she had been guilty of what I'd

accused her of, she hadn't deserved what I'd done to her. I had destroyed her, watched her crumble before my gaze. I thought she'd been lying, thought she'd been cheating on her husband, doing to him what Abigail had done to me.

Instead, she'd been running from him.

She'd been informing on his illegal activities for four years, the NCA had pushed her divorce through on the quiet because, as Rob so eloquently put it when he was tearing me a new one, *turns out, when you force a sixteen-year-old to marry, get them hooked on drugs to keep them compliant, and beat them, there's a pretty strong case for divorce.*

Her husband had beat her.

John Fucking Avery had laid his hands on her. He'd put her in hospital more than once, and not a single person had done anything about it.

She'd suffered alone for eleven years with no one to turn to, no one to trust.

The thought twisted my gut, making it hard to breathe. The heel of my hand massaged my chest as if the motion would dispel the building ache. He'd fucking hurt her. And I was no better.

I hated myself for not recognising that the bruises she arrived with had not all been from the crash. She'd been in such a mess I hadn't thought to question anything, except her intentions. Because distrust, now that burned deep, especially when she so easily seemed to navigate my defences, as if she walked a path of steppingstones straight to my heart, rather than battled against the fortified walls designed to keep others away.

If I ever got my hands on that bastard, I'd bury him. Scratch that, because by the time I was through with him there wouldn't be enough left of him to bury. No one should hurt a woman, especially not a man, we were meant to use our strength to protect, not hurt. I snort at my own thoughts. I'd fucking hurt her. I was just as guilty.

Any other time, I would have pulled some favours with the PD, but if there was one thing I knew—thanks to the evidence Grace had stashed in the surgery—it was that her ex-husband had people in his pocket all across the country. People who had sworn to protect and serve, like the knights of old, and instead had shaken off their oath to line their pockets and turn a blind eye, watching the coin, not the deed. Disgusting. Unforgivable. Just like my actions had been.

I had joined the police at eighteen, was poached by the NCA a year later for some undercover work. It had been small-time things at first, until I proved myself and was inserted into a small street gang peddling drugs in the hope to trace the money back to the person cleaning it, John Avery. How close our worlds had come to colliding. I hated to think how near I must have been to her, how, if I'd gotten a little closer, I'd have been able to do something. I would not have turned a blind eye to her pain.

No, I just caused it.

The NCA had known for years Avery was behind cleaning funds for some of the most notorious dealers. Back then, they'd thought if we could get the dirt on him, he'd give up the higher-ups to spare himself.

We'd been short-sighted. It went so much deeper than any of us had imagined, and yet we never found a scrap of evidence connecting to him.

I glanced to the binder still gripped in my hand. There was no way I was putting this down anywhere now I'd seen its contents. Grace had hidden it in the surgery, thinking no one would find it. It was probably some kind of insurance. It contained a complete breakdown of how she had moved the money and kept the trails hidden for some of the biggest names in organised crime. There were names, dates, and every penny month-to-month that had been cleaned was accounted for. We had thought John Avery seemed clean, that he was small-time at the most. We had been very, *very* wrong.

Grace's ex-husband was the linchpin in countless money laundering operations. His father's bank was barely even a blip on the radar. Looking at the files, it was no wonder even our forensic accountants couldn't trace the money. Grace was an expert. There were things in this binder that made my head spin, links that were so imaginative they wouldn't have been considered without her notes explaining them. Her notes were the codex that sent everything tumbling down.

Avery had been cautious. The accounts on their own wouldn't be enough to condemn him. For any of this to make sense they needed Grace, or these notes, which I had a feeling weren't part of the information she was handing to Jenny, the woman she had listed in the binder as her NCA contact.

What I held in my hand was a contingency plan. A way to ensure he went down even if something happened to her.

I pushed my hand through my damp hair, my vision scanning the gradient of the town, looking for some sign of her. Light drizzle misted the streets, fine droplets of rain swirling on the light mid-September breeze. What I wouldn't give to see a flash of her brown hair, the soft contours of her face, her beautiful crimson lips, clover-green eyes. I needed to know she was okay.

I pivoted as the sound of someone's

hurried approach met my ears over the roaring of the sea against the cliffs and the whisper of the rain.

"Any sign of her?" Rob asked, resting his hands on his knees to catch his breath, water dripped from his sandy coloured hair. His once perfect bedhead style now reduced to a clinging damp mop plastered against his tanned skin, framing his emerald eyes wrought with concern. I shook my head.

The knot in my stomach tightened.

I'd told her to get lost, that there was no place here for her.

And now we couldn't find her.

I'd looked everywhere from Grifters' Grove—our small collection of trees on the beach—all the way to the main road, and back again. Rob had done the same. Just half an hour ago I had seen him clambering over the boulders and rock pools that made up a natural walkway lining the cove. But there was no sign of her anywhere.

The longer we looked the more my unease festered. I'd been so blinded by rage at finding out she was married that I

# SAVING GRACE

hadn't stopped to wonder how that marriage licence had ended up on my desk in the first place. In my fury, I'd assumed someone from the town had been looking out for me. But there was no one here who would have thought to do something like that.

I had fucked up big time.

I had watched her fall apart before my gaze; broken her heart when she'd dared to trust me after everything she'd been through. I hadn't realised what a gift she had given by loving me, by letting me close. I thought I was the brave one letting *her* in, but in comparison, I was a coward.

"Have you checked her home?" Rob asked, his gaze now flitting across the beach to the cliffs, then over towards the roads. Like me, he was never still, hoping to catch a glimpse of her, some sign she was still here.

I shook my head. "Not in the last few hours."

Phoebe joined us on the beachfront, the concern of her expression mirroring our own. Her hand fought to capture her long red hair as the wind from the ocean whipped mercilessly around us.

Phoebe owned the small but famous patisserie known as $\pi r^2$ Away. With Doc sending Grace there almost every day, the two of them had just started to become close. She and Dotty had been the first people I'd checked in with. I'd really thought she would have sought comfort with one of them.

I didn't think she'd run.

Fuck. I cursed myself silently. I was such a fucking idiot. I tugged at my hair, dragging my hands down my face to feel the slight burn of my manicured scruff as I studied the streets again, praying to catch sight of her.

Nothing.

"Any sign of Andy?" Phoebe asked, concern knitting her brow. Everyone in the town called Grace, Andy, because that's what she'd asked them to do. They thought it was to keep her presence here hidden from her parents, although from what Rob said, she'd initially been hoping no one would remember her. As if she could ever be forgotten. But in my mind, I still called her Grace, still used her middle name.

Rob and I were the only ones to ever call her this. It had been our private joke because, whilst it was her middle name, she was the most accident-prone eight-year-old we'd ever met, and the way she smiled whenever we called her something other than Miranda made me want to hear that name on my lips more.

In these last few hours, I'd found out more about Grace than I was comfortable with. It was no wonder she'd hidden so much from me, no wonder she thrived on secrets. I'd known her parents were bad, but I had never imagined they would have forced their sixteen-year-old daughter to marry in order to pay off their debts to the bank. There was more to this story. More than the papers and notes told. I just hoped one day I'd get to learn it.

"I'll start knocking on doors, see if anyone's seen her. Someone must have seen her somewhere." Phoebe studied me critically for a second, crossing her arms across her willowy frame. How the owner of the best damn pie shop in the country could be so slim I didn't know. It seemed unfair, I had to use the gym in the station for an extra hour every time I even thought about her wares. "You look peaky. Get something to eat."

Eat? How could anyone be thinking of food at a time like this? I'd just found out the woman I love had been living in hell for the last eleven years. But that wasn't even the worst of it. I'd broken her and, if Rob was right, the woman who just over a month ago had been told she couldn't conceive, was carrying my child.

Pacing, I tugged at my hair again. Fuck. I had to find her. I had to make this right.

My gut spasmed, it wasn't just her I had to find. I needed to figure out who left the marriage licence on my desk in the first place because Rob was right. No one in this town would have done that, and the timing had been too opportune for me to think it was anything but planned. Someone was here who didn't belong, and they'd been watching us closely enough to know we'd argued this morning about her secrets.

They'd thrown fuel onto the fire of doubt and mistrust that burnt within me, and like a fool, I'd let it rage.

I tried to push the crushing weight of fear from my shoulders. She was here somewhere. She had to be. But that nagging doubt kept surfacing. If Grace's notes were right, and Avery had contacts in countless PDs, my check could have led him straight to her. What would a man like that do to the woman who was informing on him, to the woman he'd already turned into an addict while beating her senseless?

I dragged my hands down my face, feeling the burn of stubble.

She had to be here.

She just had to be.

## CHAPTER TWO

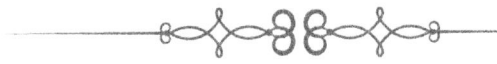

Jesse

"What is it with that woman of yours and putting eggs in the fridge?" Rob asked as I felt something heavy being draped around my shoulders. He patted my arm lightly; a nod was all I could manage as thanks. I stood on the vista near the cliffs surveying the area.

This was one of the few locations in Barrett's Bay where, if you stood in just the

# SAVING GRACE

right place, you could see almost every road in town. Barrett's Bay was built on a steep incline, the streets and houses dotted the landscape in their own kind of organised chaos, stretching right down to the road that ran adjacent to the beach.

It was the tail end of summer; the light nights were drawing to a close. The air was still warm, but the wind racing from the ocean was as cold as the dread seeping into my pores. I wrapped the jacket around me, turning to look out at the ocean as a dark thought entered my mind for what must have been the hundredth time.

"You don't think ..." I swallowed looking out at the cliffs, watching the waves crash against the rocks below. I couldn't even bring myself to say the words. My fingers pressed against my eyes as the look on her face haunted me.

Each time I replayed our last encounter in my mind I noticed more things, things that now made sense with everything I knew. I thought about the way she'd rub or scratch the flower mandala tattoo on the crook of her left arm whenever she seemed to be uncomfortable. At first, I'd thought it was a nervous habit. When she'd told me she was four years sober, I'd assumed she'd been talking about alcohol, but now this action made a lot more sense, as did the reason why she never let me run my fingers down its intricate pattern.

When she stood in reception, tears streaming down her face as she absorbed every venomous and hateful word I said, I'd been blind not to notice the red, raw scratch marks down her arm. I could see them so clearly now, burned into my vision with that look of absolute devastation.

Before I'd even torn her apart, she'd been on the edge after what had happened between us that morning.

What if ... what if I'd pushed too far? My gaze remained fixed on the rocks, praying I wouldn't see a lone sandal trapped in the currents below. I scrubbed my face, my scruff burning my palms as I applied a little too much pressure as if my discomfort would somehow help.

"I've already checked the cliffs."

Fuck. He'd thought the same thing. That's why he'd been out there earlier. I closed my eyes. Of course that's what he'd been looking for when he'd walked the rocky pathway at the cliff's base. If she'd have been sitting there, then we'd have seen her.

My mind felt as though it was filled with cotton wool, like I couldn't function. But my instincts were still intact somewhere because something Rob had just said hadn't sat right. I could feel it niggling at the back of my mind, demanding my attention. I needed to stop thinking like the arsehole who had driven the woman he loved away, and like the detective I was.

When I transferred from the NCA I had been a Senior Investigator, holding a rank equivalent to Detective Sergeant. Due to my impressive resume, when I made the transfer to the police, I was able to sit the exam and walk straight into a temporary promotion as Detective Inspector, which became permanent after twelve months. I had always suspected Abigail's father, who had connections within the precincts, was partially responsible for me finding such a position. But I was still damn good at my job. I was good at seeing the pieces, so what was I missing?

Eggs! I clicked my fingers, waving a finger at Rob as if he was privy to my thoughts and should understand the light that had just turned on full watt in my addled brain.

That was it.

I'd been teasing Grace for weeks about putting them in the fridge. She blamed it on the concussion. But now I wondered if there was more to it. "When?"

"When what?"

"When did you see the eggs in the fridge?"

"Earlier, when I stopped by to check the house. I grabbed some water from the—"

"Shit." I knew for certain she hadn't put them in there. This morning, when we'd argued, she'd left without breakfast, and I'd put them back on the side last night. My walk became a trot, then a sprint as I dashed towards her home. I was aware of

Rob following behind, the sound of his voice calling after me, but his words were lost through the roar of blood in my ears.

How had I not seen this sooner?

Someone had been in her home.

When we started spending time together, I noticed one of her habits was to unlock every door and window in her home when she was in. I'd follow her around the downstairs as she'd check each one off her list, unlocking it, opening it, and closing it again before moving on to the next.

She did this whenever she got home, and each night before bed. I'd lost count of the times I'd asked her to lock them, each time she would just offer me a slight smile and shake her head. If I'd been a virtual prisoner for eleven years, I guess I'd want to know I had an escape open too.

While they were open whenever she was in, whenever she left, they were always locked. Except today. She'd fled in such a hurry she'd left them open, and I'd locked up while trying to make sense of what I'd just seen. A bag full of cash and identification with a name other than hers on.

"Was the door locked?"

"No. Why? What's going on?" He stepped in front of me as I moved to climb the steps up the wooden entrance porch leading to the door.

"I locked it when I left." I stepped around him, opening the front door into the entrance hall, my gaze scanning the sage coloured carpet, before wandering over the pictures that ran up the wall by the stairs for the signs of anything out of place. I walked the downstairs. I had been here just this morning. Had anything changed?

My eyes trailed over the sofa and chair, across to the mantelpiece adorned with pictures of Grace, her grandparents, and even the three of us.

Nothing out of place there. Even the fine layer of dust I'd teased her about yesterday was undisturbed. One thing I came to learn quickly, Grace hated dusting, or maybe it was just something about the fireplace, because the rest of the house was completely spotless.

## SAVING GRACE

The wooden bookcases her grandfather had restored, were still stacked with books and trinkets, no dust here, so it was impossible to see if anything had been moved, but I thought everything was where it belonged. Walking through the large sliding doors into the kitchen, my eyes once more roamed. The grey marble work surfaces were clean, free of crumbs, with just the occasional streak mark from where it had been wiped down. I walked to the free-standing cabinet, running my fingers down the wood I looked into the glass display. A frown furrowing my brow.

"What are you looking for?"

"Did you put the dishes away?"

Rob shook his head. "If someone had been here, wouldn't you know? You've been living here for weeks."

"I've been an idiot," I retorted, making my way through the kitchen door that opened into the entrance hall, past the understairs toilet, and up the stairs. "I kept thinking the things she was leaving in odd places was just because of the concussion. She's been a little confused." I paced the bedroom. I knew every inch of this room by heart, so I'd barely noticed it had grown dark until Rob flicked the bedroom light on. Nothing out of place here either.

Damn. I was sure I'd been on to something.

Maybe I'm just chasing the wind.

It was *possible* she'd come home. *Maybe* she'd stashed some money from the duffel bag here and had come back for it. But the place was too clean. If she'd come back here in the state I'd left her in, her room would be a mess. At the very least, I'd expect a drawer or cupboard to be turned out or left open.

Rob flicked the light off as we left the room. My fingers tangled in my hair again as I turned back to the place I had spent so many nights holding her. I blinked as a small glint of light beneath the bed caught my attention. I followed the glow letting it guide me like the Christmas star, because a star was exactly what it was.

Crouching, I turned it over in my fingers before lifting my gaze towards the royal blue ceiling. Looking at the soft glow of the countless constellations we'd mapped out on the ceiling when we were twelve.

I closed my eyes, trying to remember them, trying to think where this fallen star belonged. Red lit my eyelids as Rob flicked the light on, breaking my concentration.

"Jesse," Rob's voice was grave. He was staring up. "Is there a reason there's a hole in the ceiling?" It was almost invisible, lost in the dark shades of the paint. If not for knowing the exact place to look, thanks to the fallen star, I never would have seen it.

Hell, I'd spent hours lying in this room, looking at the ceiling, and I'd never noticed. Then again, my attention had been elsewhere. When Grace was in the room, everything outside of her faded from focus. There was only her. I could lie for hours, just inhaling her scent and listening to the sound of her breathing. When she was with me, I'd wanted nothing more than to spend the rest of my life making her smile. Instead, I'd torn her apart, ripped her down when I should have been building her up.

"Shit!" The curse dropped from my lips in a growl as I stalked towards her grandparents' room. Upstairs had always been spared her locking, unlocking routine. In all the time we'd been together, I'd not seen her go in the room once. Although, the fact she'd thanked my parents for dealing with her grandparents' clothes meant she must have been in there at one point. I bet she left the windows upstairs unlocked. No one in the right mind would try to squeeze in through those tiny windows and holding a ladder against the house was a sure-fire way to get tongues wagging. Just last month I'd been called out to a peeping Tom, only to discover the regular window cleaner had taken ill and had sent his business partner on his rounds in his place. The poor guy had turned scarlet as I questioned him.

The back room lacked the bay window of the front, and instead of looking out over the cove, looked up at the town. I allowed my gaze to study the houses opposite, the view inside other people's homes obscured by nets and blinds. Depressing the button on the window handle I gave it a push. Unlocked. Just as I suspected. Not that it told me anything, only a child would fit through this kind of gap.

I glanced around the room, reminding myself of the layout. A large double bed was placed against the internal wall, still covered in the dust cloths Mum had placed on them when she emptied the house. There was another cover over the small vanity near the door, and the two wardrobes stood slightly ajar to keep them aired.

I followed the windowsill, already seeing what was amiss. The loft hatch in these cottages was usually placed in a built-in wardrobe, but Grace's gramps had taken out the walls, so it was found directly above the small bedside table. He'd painted it closed when Grace's gran complained about the draft.

Black score lines traced the square shape of the hatch, the flecks of paint mocking me on the dust covers. If I'd come in here, I would have noticed this, I would have looked.

Standing on the table I pushed myself up, the slick oil of the wood shimmered on my fingers as I pushed the seal upwards, gliding the hatch open, pushing it across onto the floor. I rubbed my fingers together, bringing it to my nose. Olive oil. I didn't like this one bit.

"Pass me your phone." I curled my fingers at Rob, waiting as he fished inside his jacket. Flicking his phone to flashlight, I swept the light through the dark hole. A partial floor had been put down, originally because they'd been planning to convert it into another room, but the job had been left half-finished. "What the fuck?"

I wasn't sure what emotion slammed me first—rage, frustration, fury—but it was some form of anger, and it felt like a solid blow. In the attic were blankets, discarded water bottles, and a plate Grace had been looking for just a few days ago. The air hung heavy with the sour scent of stale bread.

"What do you see?"

"Some mother fucker's been watching her. They've been living in the same damn house." I pushed myself up into the cavity, being careful not to disturb the scene. Training overpowered common sense because I knew, even as I placed each step carefully on the boards, that there was no one I could trust to handle this scene. I didn't know who to trust. While I had the names of potentially dirty cops, there was no telling who their friends were, and even if their friends weren't crooked, there was no way to be sure word wouldn't reach unwanted ears.

Pinpricks of light shone from below, I edged forward, my gut churning at all the spy holes. Discarded crisp packets and half-eaten loaves were scattered across the floor near a pile of rumpled blankets. There were even the yellow stains of egg yolk on the discarded plate. How long had this fucker been here? How had he even found this place without being seen?

"What do we do now?" Rob asked as I descended the attic.

I pushed a hand through my hair. "I don't know, we sure as hell can't go to the police."

Think. Damn it, if I could just have kept my mouth shut Grace wouldn't have felt the need to run. She wouldn't have been alone. This wouldn't have happened. No matter what I hoped, the discarded camp here pointed to one thing and one thing only. Someone had known Grace was here, and I seriously doubted that she left by her own volition.

## CHAPTER THREE

### Miranda

I have mantras. Words that once gave me strength. When I was fighting against the pull of my addiction, I would focus on my breathing, repeat them, and eventually find my resolve. The itch that burned beneath my skin would fade and become something other than all-consuming. Tolerable. Never gone, but manageable.

Those words were my salvation.
But they aren't working.
*Nothing* is working.

Because every time I try to find my calm, I see his face. It's burned into my mind. Every time I blink, every time I breathe, I see him looking at me with disgust. With hatred. My ears buzz with the sound of his voice. The man who had held me in his arms, fixed me without even knowing I was broken, had destroyed me more completely than John ever had. The venom of his words, mingled with the burn beneath my skin, was driving me to madness.

My arms were raw, bleeding from the way I sank my nails deep into my skin seeking just a minute of release.

I thought I'd known pain, but nothing had prepared me for this. My heart ached, stifling my breath as my fingertips massaged the small bag of white powder John had left me with after locking me in this small room with white walls, and a bricked-up window. He'd even removed the mirror and door from the bathroom.

I had spent eleven years with John, was forced to marry him at sixteen so my parents could keep their house and clear the debt my sister left behind when she overdosed. He'd been hounding me for years. I had felt an icy shiver across my skin each and every time his eyes would find me. I hadn't wanted to marry him. I hadn't even wanted to be near him.

After one of my many rejections, he had turned his sights on my sister, Dana, getting close to her as a way to get to me. It had been he who had first introduced her to drugs, and his father had done the same with me on the day I became a bride.

I don't remember my wedding day. I remember my father dragging me down the stairs, restraining me while Mr Avery injected me with something. Everything else was just vague impressions and echoing voices, until I awoke in the honeymoon suite.

I tried to run, to escape the man I'd never wanted to kiss let alone marry, so to keep me in line they made me dependent on them. Got me hooked. And after they were certain I was controllable, that I was too afraid, too weak, to try to run again, they reduced the dose, keeping me functioning, in line, and always crawling back to them for more.

    I had done things to get that next fix I wasn't proud of, things that still make me sick to the stomach.

    I'd always been brilliant at maths. I'd been planning to go to college and become an accountant, and thanks to the joys of Open University, and John's contacts, they had ensured I would be of use to them. I became a high-functioning addict, able to complete my tasks, but always chasing that high.

    Someone had seen my potential, ensured I was trained to the highest standard. I knew the world of forensic accounting inside and out, knew how to avoid their money being traced and detected. The whole thing just clicked. Which was why, after I took over, the trails hinting at their involvement stopped. I was damn good at my job. I had to be because some days I felt like it was the only thing keeping me alive.

    Four years ago, John decided it was time I produced an heir to the empire he had built. I was forced through violent withdrawal and rehab. It was there I met Jenny. At first, I thought she was like me, it was only when I came to depend on her she revealed her true nature.

I should have known she was using me. People only got close to me when they wanted something. They never wanted me because, as my parents had made clear, I was never enough. I was the child they hadn't wanted. A drain on time and resources.

Jenny was part of a small team in the NCA who were trying to gather evidence against John in order to bring him in, hoping they could offer him a deal to implicate some big players they suspected his paths crossed. They hadn't realised how big he was in his world.

John laundered money. And with my help on the accounting side, his operations had grown. He cleaned money for more organisations than I dared to imagine. Except I didn't need to imagine, because I knew the name of every single one, how much money they moved each month, and the ways we diverted it for cleaning. I even knew who was being paid to look the other way. It was all there, in my ledgers, encrypted and coded, even John couldn't decipher my books, but as long as he knew where everything was, down to the last penny, he didn't care.

In exchange for immunity for my involvement—unwilling as it was—I began to gather evidence. I knew even as I passed copies of my handwritten ledgers off to Jenny that, without me, they would make no sense. It was the only card I had to bargain with. My insurance policy to make sure they kept their word about getting me away from him.

I needed to make sure I was safe. She promised me witness protection when they had enough information. But when the time came, her superiors denied her request. I think they had wanted me to stay there longer, until I could give them something that didn't centre around me being a witness.

Just before I ran, John had put me in hospital. It wasn't the first time, and I knew if I stayed it wouldn't be the last. But this time had been different. Danny Tavott—the American Doctor who John had brought over to fill a position in the hospital—had just informed us that I couldn't have children, that I wouldn't be able to provide John with the heir he so desperately wanted.

He'd almost killed me that night.

Probably would have if Bastian hadn't come home. I remember being curled up on the kitchen floor, his boot being driven repeatedly into my stomach. Bastian's was the last voice I'd heard before I blacked out and woke up in hospital.

While there, Jenny had visited, sneaking me a fake ID and the divorce papers they'd been promising me for years. They told me they'd suppressed the paperwork so John wouldn't know. For my safety, no one could discover what they had done, but I was no longer married and that had been all that mattered.

I don't know if it was because the witness protection deal had fallen through, or because she knew if I stayed John was likely to kill me and they'd lose my testimony, but she told me to run. To tell no one but Bastian where I was, and she'd get word to me through him when they had John in custody and needed to make arrangements for me to testify.

I had met Bastian several times over the years before he came to live with us. Mr Avery insisted on having family gatherings, but I'd known better than to talk with him. Besides, at the time, the guy had hated my guts. If looks could kill, the lasers he directed towards me would have had extinction event potential.

But that all changed just over a year ago. One day he had been the man I only saw in passing as I played the doting wife, the next he was living under the same roof as me, a face like thunder and an attitude to match.

He'd taken an instant dislike to me. I already knew his secrets, I'd hidden the trail that pointed to him, but I was the wife of his half-brother, the man who was threatening his younger brother and sister if he didn't bend to John's will. And John's will, after Mr Avery had been reported dead in a boating accident, was to finally have his brother living under the same roof, where we could be a proper family.

John believed family was loyal. Bastian thought anyone who would choose to marry a man like John had to be as rotten as his brother. I couldn't blame him. I'd become so good at faking that, some days, even I hadn't known where the act began.

John hid the abuse well. Rarely bruising me where it could be seen, but it wasn't just the bruises, it was the mind games. He excelled in torture. Whenever he took things too far, he had Danny in the perfect position in the hospital to ensure no one raised any flags. Even when he lost control, I knew how to use make-up to hide. I knew not to embarrass him.

I still remember the day I saw the first hint of softness in Bastian's eyes. I'd sat shivering in the bedroom, waiting to hear the lock engage on the front door to tell me John had left. I was always locked in, only allowed outside when he granted me that privilege and, even then, he had me followed.

Thinking I was alone, I'd crawled from the bedroom to the bathroom, where I hid my first-aid supplies. John didn't like them in the en-suite. The reminder of what I made him do to me only fuelled his aggression, so I'd quickly learnt where to hide things out of sight. And I got damn good at cleaning up blood.

My head had been pounding so much, that I'd mistaken the sound of the shower for the roar of static. I'd barely dragged myself inside when I passed out. When I came around, Bastian was leaning over me, dripping wet, wrapped in nothing more than a towel, pressing a cold compress to my swollen cheek. And I'd panicked.

I'd pushed myself under the sink, mentally checking I hadn't been touched. John made it clear he was the only one ever allowed to be inside me, and I knew there would be severe consequences if I was ever sullied. I was his alone.

As if understanding my fear, he'd dragged his jeans up his damp body, yanked me out from under the sink, and cradled me on the bathroom floor, my ass between his crossed legs as he cleaned my wounds using the kit I'd taped beneath the toilet tank. I think this was the first time anyone had seen my fear. In honesty, it was probably the first time anyone had tried to see me as something other than a trophy wife. It was easier to believe everything was as it appeared, rather than scratch at the surface of a golden statue to see the clay beneath. After that, the two of us had grown close, beyond the pretence John had made us endure.

I thought back to Bastian's words as he'd escorted me to this room. He told me we'd fix this. But this was not something that could be remedied. I knew he cared. We'd built a friendship outside the sight of John's men. But there was nothing he could do, not without putting his family at risk. His brother and sister were innocent. They had a whole future ahead of them. Helping me would not be worth the trade. He had to see this. Helping me had no value because I had no worth.

It seemed like a lifetime ago since

Doctor Danny Tavott grasped my arm on the beachfront and gave me the ultimatum. I either returned home willingly, or he would tell John about Fate, tell him I'd been sullied, and he, and everyone who had helped me, would pay.

There wasn't a choice. Fate may despise me, he may have broken my heart, but all my best memories were of him. To save the man I love, I returned to the man who claimed to love me.

John's love was violent, toxic, but it seemed to be the only kind I was worthy of. I guess I'd always known, deep in my heart, that this was all I deserved. There was something wrong with me, and it spread right down into my soul, making me unwanted, unlovable. Worthless.

I caressed the bag in my fingers. Pinching and squeezing, watching the hypnotic way the white powder moved inside. There was something seductive about the way the light played on the bag, how the powder clumped and crumbled beneath my touch, begging me to taste it. Needing me.

## SAVING GRACE

I blinked slowly, trying to push away the demons.
*I gain the strength of the temptation I resist.*
*This is my choice.*
*I am strong.*
*Tough people last longer than tough times.*
I mentally repeated my mantras.
But another voice was louder.
*'It's no wonder you'll never be enough for anyone, you're disgusting.'*
*'Get lost, Andy. There's no place for people like you here.'*
It echoed in time with that voice in my mind, the one which always told me I would never be enough, never be good enough, never amount to anything or deserve anything good. I always thought this voice should sound like my mother, but it didn't. It sounded like me, and it brought to the surface all my deepest fears.

My chest ached; tears burned. I was just so damn tired. Where once strength burnt in my core, my will to fight and carry on once nestled, there was only a gaping hollow pit that threatened to consume me.

I had tried. I had known happiness for a moment, knew what it was to feel like everyone else. But such things would always be my unreachable star, and anything I seized turned to dust and crumbled in my toxic hands because I wasn't worthy enough to hold on to it.

I was never enough.

Tears rolled from my eyes, caught in my hands, turning the bag within my grasp damp.

I was tired of fighting. Tired of the voices. Tired of struggling through each and every second. For one moment, in Barrett's Bay, I had dared to hope for something better. But being brought back here had been the spear driven through the chink in my armour. The killing blow. I couldn't do this again. I wasn't strong enough.

For the last four years, the hope of leaving here had been all that kept me going, knowing that there was an end in sight, that as soon as I gave the NCA what they needed I would be free, and I'd never again have to lay eyes on this hellhole. But now there was nothing. No hope, nothing.

What was the point of fighting, when the only thought that kept me going had evaporated like a snowflake in the fires of Hell?

I was out of hope, but maybe I could still find comfort.

I stared at the bag in my hand, tears streaking my face.

Four years. I'd fought my addiction for four long years, and my resolve had broken in mere minutes.

My mantras made one last desperate attempt to reach me. But as my gaze fixed upon the promise of obscurity, only one penetrated my consciousness.

*This is my choice.*

Maybe I'd fought long enough.

Oblivion was better.

This room, these four tiny walls, would drive me mad. I knew now why the window was bricked up, why the mirror had been removed, and only a mattress lay on the highly polished floor. There was nothing here; nothing but my thoughts, and my mind was not a good place, because all I kept coming back to was the bag in my hand and the hatred in his voice.

My trembling fingers ran the length of the zip seal, thumb and forefinger occasionally pinching the tip, tugging a little. Fighting both to open it and keep it sealed.

I couldn't give John the one thing he wanted.

I was going to die here.

Why not make it my own choice, why not spare myself the pain?

I heard the crack of the seal, my choking sobs as I surrendered to the demon that had plagued me for four long years.

A sweet smell filled the air as dust rose from the bag.

Dust?

Sweet smell?

Fucking bastard!

I screamed in frustration. The sobs and wails echoed around the small room as my violently trembling hand threw the bag at the wall. The white powder exploded with a puff of sweet-tasting smoke as I collapsed sideways onto the floor in heaving sobs. Barbed wire coiled around my chest, squeezing and crushing each pained sob from my raw body.

Why wouldn't he just let me die?

"That was rude. I thought you liked sherbet powder." I heard the bolt on the door slide as John's voice penetrated the sound of my wails. The light from the hallway made his golden hair shimmer as he stood in the doorway, looking down on me. The bastard had been watching me. He gathered me into his arms, holding me while I trembled and sobbed. His hands traced through my long brown hair with such affection that, if it wasn't for the fact he was a heartless, twisted bastard, it could be mistaken for love, rather than just another tool of manipulation. "Come now, I've got you. I'll protect you." He continued to soothe me, hold me in his warm embrace.

Fire burned beneath my skin; my teeth chattered through sobs I couldn't calm. I'd resigned myself to surrender only to have my escape snatched away. I was weak, a coward, and I hated that, as he embraced me through the raw and savage destruction coursing through me, part of me felt relieved to be held in someone's arms.

## CHAPTER FOUR

### Miranda

Someone was touching me, brushing their fingers softly through my hair as I stirred from sleep. My body felt heavy in the way it always did after I'd been crying. The memory of earlier came rushing back, slamming into me with all the force of a solid blow. Stealing my breath.

My eyes shot open. I was expecting the white-washed walls, but nothing had prepared me for the sight of a red salvia on the mattress. Just the sight of it made it live up to its name of red arrow, because it felt like a shot to my heart. My heart constricted painfully. John always left me this flower. From what I saw in the photos, my wedding bouquet had been trimmed with it. It was just another declaration. Forever mine. I felt his fingers thread through my hair again, my body jolted, wrought with tension at the realisation he lay behind me.

Oh God.

All that had really happened. The temptation, the surrender, being held in his arms until I was too exhausted to keep my eyes open.

I tried to turn my head from his touch, but he just shushed me, cupping my cheek with his palm. My arm rose, ready to swat him away before I let it fall back to the mattress. Was there even any point in fighting?

"Come on now, rise and shine, baby. Doctor Tavott's here, he's got some good news." With a sharp tug he pulled me onto my back, and kissed the corner of my mouth, his eyes flashing with anger as I pushed myself away from him awkwardly.

## SAVING GRACE

The movement only made my head spin and nausea burn in the pit of my stomach. I swallowed the bitter bile, my eyes wide, never leaving him. When trapped with a predator you never take your eyes off them.

It was hard to think a man who would be at home on the cover of a magazine, could be forged from darkness. His hair was golden, and he had the smooth-shaven face of an angel, with pleasing angles that hummed of masculinity. But Lucifer had once been an angel too. Darkness came wrapped in pretty packages to keep its prey calm. But I saw past his strong physique, his God-sent features. He was a monster. And his muscles were taut, brown eyes warning he was waiting to pounce.

His hand fastened around my wrist, tugging me back against him. "You must be hungry. But before I let you eat, tell me, why did you leave me?"

This was it. The moment that defined how my life would be. I needed to appease him. "I ... I disappointed you," I sniffled. I could fake anything, right now, my instincts were telling me I had to sell this story. "I'm your wife," I swallowed again, ignoring the vile taste of the words. I hated how weak and pathetic my voice sounded, how I felt in his presence. "I can't give you the only thing you wanted." The tears were real, but they weren't for him. "I thought ... I thought if I was dead then you'd move on, find someone who could—" He silenced me with a kiss, his lips the same nauseating combination of bitter coffee and brandy I recalled.

"Oh, baby, surely you know it's you I want." He kissed me again, harder, sinking his teeth into my lip when they remained clamped together. Hands clenched at my side, I tried to stay calm, control the panic that consumed me. Easing my hands between us I pushed him away, getting to my feet. I saw his anger spike as he rose to stalk towards me. He took a slow, deep breath as if to calm himself.

"But I can't give you what you want. You'd be better with someone else."

His fists tightened, the sound of his grinding teeth sending a prickle chasing across my skin. "There will *never* be anyone else. I meant what I said Miranda, I'll love you to death." Not until death, to death, those words had always resonated within me. I believe them with every ounce of my being. I gasped, feeling the wall against my back. My pulse quickening in time with my short, panting breaths, realising I'd let him corner me.

"Please, you don't want me. You can do better." He stepped forward, I flinched, expecting him to hit me, but the blow never came. His maple eyes fixed to mine and I could see the rage burning within them, see how hard he was holding himself back. Three slow breaths left him. It was actually scarier watching him fight his beast than when he struck out without warning.

"I get it, baby, I do. You need time to adjust. But you're home now, everything is going to be fine."

"How can everything be fine? I can't give you what you want!" I could feel my hysteria rising, my nails digging into the wall to feel the smooth brick hidden beneath the white paint. "You're keeping me locked in here, in this room, fucking with me—" Pain burst in a flash of white light across my cheek as he backhanded me mid-rant. My hand flew to cup my face, feeling the angry heat against my palm and the taste of blood in my mouth as it trickled from my lip. What had I been thinking? I didn't speak to John like this. There was a second of silence, he clenched his fist, raising his hand to send it ploughing forward to punch the wall beside me. I shrank, pushing myself further into the wall as if it could protect me.

"Fuck! For God's sake, Miranda! Stop it. Stop pushing me!" His voice was razor-sharp. "I'm trying to be the bigger fucking man here. You ran from me. *No-one* runs from me." He dragged his hands down his face before he reached out to touch me. I flinched, but he'd never let that deter him. He pulled my hand from my face, running his fingertips over the place he'd struck me. "I'm sorry, baby. I didn't mean to hit you."

*Then why do you keep doing it?*

"You just have to stop pushing me."

"I'm sorry. I—" His fist slammed into

the wall again, making me jump, my chest heaving like a rabbit caught in a hunter's sights.

"I came to tell you good news, and this," he gestured towards me, "this is what I get?" He closed the space between us, caging me in, growling as I turned my head from his kiss. What was wrong with me, did I have a death wish? He grabbed my chin, yanking my head back towards him, forcing his tongue into my mouth. I tried to push away from the wall, but he kept me there, pinned. His hands roughly re-familiarising themselves with my body.

I felt trapped, suffocated. Claustrophobia closed in around me making it impossible to breathe. I brought my hands up, trying to ease him back so I could catch a breath, but he grabbed them, pinning them painfully above my head, moving so one of his enormous hands held both of mine in place.

"Don't fight me on this, baby." He pressed his cock against my stomach. "Can't you see I want you? This should be all the reassurance you need." He ground against me, making sure I felt the way his erection strained against the fabric of his black trousers. "Stop fighting me and just feel how much I love you." I tugged against his grip, but he only increased the pressure until I swear I felt the bones bending in my wrist. "Do I need to prove it? What will it take for you to see I still want you?"

I cried as he grabbed my hair, dragging my back from the wall. My legs were weak, stumbling beneath me as he pulled me towards the mattress. Oh God.

"If this is what it will take, I'll prove it to you, show you how much I want you."

Fear washed over me. I was used to being his wife, accepting the role asked of me. But this felt different. Fear bubbled inside me. Why hadn't I been able to just fake it, show John what he'd needed to see? Perhaps because I'd known freedom, known what it felt like to give myself to someone completely.

*Yeah, but he hates you. He never loved you. He's probably forgotten you already.*

The voice was right. Fate had probably not given me a second thought. Hell, he was probably overjoyed to discover I'd gone. He told me to leave, he wouldn't blink twice at my absence, if he even noticed I was gone at all.

Too quickly I felt the mattress against my back as I was pinned beneath him. My wrists fastened above my head while his free hand fought with his trousers, his knees digging painfully between my thighs, pushing my legs apart.

"I'll show you, baby. You're mine. I'll never let you doubt it again." I felt the heat of his erection between my legs and whimpered, pressing my eyes closed. He brushed a kiss to my lips, misinterpreting the sound for one of need. "That's right, baby. Tavott said you stayed clean, but that's not the news I wanted to surprise you with." He kissed his way towards my ear. "He's found a fertility treatment he's certain will work. You'll have my baby after all." I cried out as he forced himself inside me, kissing my tears away. "See, baby. Everything will be okay. You're home now."

## CHAPTER FIVE

### Jesse

"Toothpaste, in the Oreos! Seriously, Doc, that's too far, man. Too far!" I heard Doc's belly laugh rumbling through the surgery in response to my brother's cry of outrage.

I knew she wasn't there, but my eyes still gravitated towards the reception, hoping to see the sway of her brown hair, a flash of those mesmerising, clover-green eyes that caused my pulse to race. My chest ached with the need to catch just one more glimpse of her, to know she was okay. Her absence was like an all-consuming void, gnawing away at me from the inside.

I was sleeping on her side of the bed, breathing in her scent each night, like a love-sick teenager, reminding myself I had done this. Every noise, every creak and groan of the cottage, would have me snapping to attention, hoping against the odds she had come home. I used to scold her for leaving the doors unlocked, now I was doing the same thing while I was there, just hoping she'd come back.

It was a fool's hope. I knew she wasn't coming home. Not without help, because I now knew she hadn't been alone the last time someone had seen her. Jason, a teacher at the school in the neighbouring town, had seen her with someone near the beach. He'd been driving along the coast road during his lunch break to pick up the homework assignments he'd forgotten that morning. The thing was the man he described seeing her with didn't sound like Avery.

The humour in Rob's eyes died the moment he saw me. "Jesse." He acknowledged me curtly. I hated the way he was looking at me. When Abigail broke my heart, it had been Rob I went to, and he had supported me through everything, kept me from sinking. I had been hurt and angry, but it was the quiet kind of hurt that festered inside, containable. I couldn't contain this, it leaked from my every pore to become palpable.

Rob had been furious at me for what I'd done to Grace. It's the first time I think he's ever looked like he really wanted to punch me. I wouldn't have blamed him if he had. I sure as hell deserved it. I would have let him too. I would have taken every blow he'd dealt without protest. Instead, he'd turned his back to me and walked away.

Even when he was in med school, we'd always maintained a close relationship. This distance, the way he looked at me now, was eating me up inside. The silence was worse than any punch he could have thrown. Since finding out she didn't leave alone, he'd barely even made eye contact with me. I knew what he was thinking because I was thinking it too. If I hadn't acted the way I did, she wouldn't have been vulnerable. Rob avoided me with ease. Made sure we were never at our parents' house at the same time. The only time we even spoke anymore was when I told him what I knew.

Right now, the only thing I knew was that I needed Grace. I needed to hold her, to take her in my arms, breathe in her scent and know she was okay. But I didn't even know if she was still alive. And these were the thoughts that consumed me.

It was killing me that all I could do was wait. I called my old partner at the NCA, trying to track down this Jenny woman Grace had mentioned in the files. She had to know something; she had to, especially since I'd finally given up and looked at her background check. The file was suspiciously thin given what I knew. But that wasn't the worst of it. The worst was seeing the big red stamp with the word deceased, over her picture. I'd stared at those red letters until my eyes burned. Until every time I blinked, I saw the after image of that word.

She had been reported dead the day she turned up in Barrett's Bay.

"Any news?" My mind had strayed, I hadn't even realised Rob was now standing beside me, that same concerned look in his green eyes. He placed his hand on my shoulder as if it would give me strength. It was the first compassion he had shown me for a week, and I nearly caved. He would never know what that simple touch had meant. Unable to find my voice, I shook my head.

He didn't speak again, after a moment the warmth of his touch receded, and we were once again two strangers in a room. This silence was killing me. I wasn't even sure why I was here. No, that was a lie. I knew exactly what had brought me to these doors today.

She'd been missing a week, and I knew I was just torturing myself, finding a way to drive the knife in deeper and hurt myself more, but I had to know. "Did her blood test results come back?"

The way his face contorted was all the answer I needed. I grabbed my phone from my pocket, hitting redial, already pacing. It answered on the second ring.

"Holt."

"Aaron, Jesse." I swear I heard him sigh. With the exception of Dale, Aaron had been my closest friend. He was my partner at the NCA. We'd stayed in touch, but when I'd discovered Abigail was cheating on me, our contact tapered off.

"You find anything?"

"There was a team. They were reassigned when their star witness died."

"She's not dead," I growled. She better *not* be dead, but what if—I shook my head. I couldn't go down that path, couldn't afford to dwell on that train of thought. But it was too late, because the knots in my gut twisted to painful proportions, stealing what little breath I'd managed to draw into my lungs. My hand clamped around the back of the waiting room chair until it groaned in protest to my crushing grasp. If Avery had discovered she was an informant, she very well could be.

I dragged a hand through my hair, tugging it as it passed between my fingers.

This was all my fucking fault. I drove her away. I did this. Whatever happened to her was on me.

"Riiight." He drew the word out a little too long for my liking. I imagine he'd seen the same file as me, the same DNA report that showed her body had been recovered from the scene. "Anyway, I tracked down this Jenny and passed your details on to her. But ... Jesse."

"I know." He didn't need to tell me not to get my hopes up, holding onto even a single thread of hope was getting more impossible by the day.

## Jesse

I stared at the screen. I don't even know what I was meant to be doing. While I was based in Barrett's Bay, my actual area included all the small towns that were nestled along this stretch of coast. It was almost enough to keep anyone busy, but I just couldn't focus.

The bell sounded, my vision snapping up from the polished counter to see an unfamiliar woman. Her honey-blonde hair had been secured in a high ponytail. The combination of smart shirt and skirt, coupled with the way her brown eyes assessed me through her fashionable glasses, told me all I needed to know.

Pulse quickening, I straightened. I prayed I was right, begged I wasn't jumping to conclusions. "Jenny?"

"DI Fateson?" Although it was a question, I could tell she must have at least pulled my file. This woman knew exactly who I was.

"Jesse, please." She nodded as I gestured towards the seat opposite me. The leather of the virtually unused seat creaked as she lowered her slender frame into it, her body language open, confident as she watched me.

"I hear you've been trying to reach me. Tell me, why does a small-town DI feel the need to send an errand boy to find me, when a call to head office would have confirmed my location?"

"I don't know who to trust." She hiked an eyebrow, inviting me to continue, but otherwise, her expression remained schooled. I turned my monitor towards her, pulling up Grace's file. It was then, as her gaze passed over the screen, that I saw the first real flash of emotion across her features. Grief. The woman hadn't just been her contact, she'd cared for Grace. Her eyes lingered on the picture a little too long as she stared, almost as if not trusting herself to blink.

Fuck. This woman was in mourning.

"What does Miranda Avery have to do with why you were looking for me?" Her voice remained steady, but I saw the way her hands bunched the fabric of her skirt. A tell, which was an unusual thing for someone in her line of work. Seeing Grace's picture had thrown her off centre, and that took a hell of a lot of doing when this woman's life depended on the signals her body would give. Or maybe she was playing me, letting me see what she thought I needed to. I hated undercover operatives. You couldn't trust even the simplest of gestures.

"You were her contact, right?" I could

see from her expression she needed more. She was like me, didn't know who could be trusted. "She was informing on her hu—ex-husband." I could see that got her attention. Her gaze snapped towards the door, before studying the small office space. "Accounts, names, contacts, she mapped the whole operation for you. There was just one issue. She handled the accounts so well even your team of forensic accountants couldn't crack the pattern without her."

"I'll bite. What else do you know?"

"I know Avery has police in his pockets, that he's running a money-laundering operation of the likes you've probably not uncovered before, and I know for a fact, she didn't die in this crash." I clicked on the incident report, bringing up pictures of the totalled car.

My stomach did a backflip, the same way it had when I first saw the twisted, burnt out hunk of metal. Grace had been inside that car. From what the reports said, there was evidence the airbags had failed, and the brakes had been tampered with.

Her death was being treated as a murder, and the number one suspect was a woman called Ana, Avery's sister, who had been caught on camera heading towards the place the car had been parked, which had been outside the camera's field of vision.

I still can't believe she walked away from that.

"Can you prove it?" There was something suspiciously like hope in her voice, and I gave it a moment to wash over me. Hope was in short supply these days.

"Which part? That she didn't die? I have a town full of people who will confirm she stayed here for a month before vanishing."

"Vanishing?" I heard her swallow, the quiver in her voice. How much of this act was real? What if I was making things worse, what if Jenny wasn't who Grace thought she had been? No, I couldn't think like this, she was NCA. Aaron had tracked her down himself.

"I went to her funeral," she whispered. "Damn him. I honestly thought ..." Her fists clenched and slackened several times.

Then as if realising she'd given something away, she schooled her features once more. Too late. She'd been leaking emotion since first seeing Grace's picture. "*If* what you say is true, why reach out to me?"

"She trusted you. But you have to have other contacts, someone who can confirm if she's—" I swallowed, unable to bring myself to say the word. I needed to know what we were dealing with. Needed a plan. "What's the risk to Andy if she's back with him?" Using this name made her relax further. It seemed I'd proven I knew enough to be trusted, but I wasn't willing to tip my hand. I wouldn't reveal the existence of the footnoted files. If I did, there would be no reason for them to put any resources into finding her. I needed them looking for her. I needed her to come home.

"Avery didn't know she was informing. But the guy was obsessed. I'm talking full-on stalker with abusive tendencies. In the four years since our paths crossed, I lost count of the times the doctor came out. She didn't tell me the whole story, but the things I do know ..." She shook her head. "What is she to you?"

"Everything." Every-damn-thing. She seemed taken aback by my declaration, or maybe it was the way I held her gaze, forcing the sincerity of my words to resonate within her.

"Look, I'll see what I can do. I'll have to prove life, which means I need to get permission to exhume the body. That could take weeks."

She was right, and there was another problem with her plan. If Avery thought for one minute anyone was questioning who lay in the coffin, he might very well cover his tracks by giving them a real corpse. "Give me a minute."

I pulled my phone out. Bile churning in my stomach as I listened to the phone ring. It may as well have been the shriek of a banshee given the effect it had on me. My skin prickled, jaw clenched so hard it was a wonder my gums weren't bleeding.

"Jesse?" Abigail seemed confused. No wonder. I *never* called her. Anything I wanted to say to her, I did through Rob unless she called me directly.

My mouth turned dry, but pride would never stop me from this. "I need your help."

"Why would *I* help *you?* You deliberately made it difficult for Dale to—"

"I'll give you the house."

There was a stunned silence on the line as she no doubt questioned if she'd heard correctly. She knew what that place meant to me. It had been in my family for generations. My mother had been raised in that house, my brother had been born on the kitchen floor.

It was a place filled with memories and joy. We used to spend every Christmas there, right up until my Nan died. The house had needed work; it was old, run-down, and although she'd had the money for repairs, she'd wanted to leave it exactly as it was. She'd left it between us in her will, and I'd bought my parents and brother out with the money she had left us, since they decided they wanted to sell. I'd been sixteen at the time.

It was thanks to this house, and the

Internet, I learnt how to repair things. I started working as a cop at eighteen, and I sank every free minute I had into restoring it. I lived in it, with cold water and broken heating, even when the NCA took me on. Grace's Gramps even stopped by the occasional weekend, helping me pull up old uneven floorboards and giving me the kind of tips only an experienced joiner knew.

By the time I started my short undercover gig at twenty-one, the house had been finished. I decided to rent it out as a source of extra income and move to another city to be closer to my job. I met Abigail when I was twenty-two, and we married within six months.

She hadn't known about the house until two years later when we were looking for somewhere to move back to our home city, which had timed perfectly with the fact my tenants had moved out three months before.

Whenever a tenant left, I had the place stripped, new carpets fitted, and every room redecorated, so the place was pristine before the removal company even arrived.

She had fallen in love with the house at first sight and wanted to know why I had never mentioned it before. I hadn't been keeping it from her, but with it always having a tenant in, I hadn't given it much thought.

I loved that house. It was a piece of history. It was the only place I'd imagined raising children, the kind of house you grew old in, surrounded by love, laughter, and family. Many of my dreams had centred around it, but now they only centred around Grace. What use were bricks and mortar if the one person I wanted to build that future with was lost?

"What do you need?"

"I need you to call your father. I need something pushed through on the quiet—"

"I'm not doing anything illegal," she snapped, haughtily. I hung my head, my gaze burning into the navy carpet tiles. Had this woman ever even known me at all?

"It's nothing illegal," I bit back the anger as best I could. "Someone I care about is in trouble, and I don't know who can be trusted if the wrong people get wind of what's happening."

"Is Rob okay?" The concern in her voice for my brother stung a little. She'd always liked him, perhaps even cared for him more than me. I suspected that she'd maybe even tried to seduce him at one point. I wouldn't have put it past her, especially knowing what I did now. He'd made his dislike for her known even before we were married. He refused to be my best man; told me I was making a mistake.

I should have listened.

"He's fine."

"Then who—"

"Do you want the house or not?"

"You know I do." I did. Whenever we spoke, she always asked what I would part with it for. Because of the baby, which I'd thought was mine at the time, I'd agreed she could stay there rent-free until I was ready to move in. It was the one thing she had touched that I had still wanted to keep, until now.

"Have your father call me. If he agrees,

I'll sign the deeds over to you." I felt the slight crack in my voice.

"Jesse, is everything okay?" The genuine concern in her voice took me by surprise. She hadn't shown an ounce of compassion for years, she'd just taken. She had realised long before I had our marriage would fail, but whereas I tried harder to make things work, ensure she wanted for nothing, she cast me off, seeking pleasures in different waters.

"No. Just, have your father call me. Please." I ended the call before she could say anything else.

"You were serious." Jenny was regarding me curiously over the top of her glasses. "About what she means to you. But tell me D.I. Fateson, whose favour is worth giving up your home for? And who exactly were you talking to?"

"My ex-wife, Abigail Weatherford."

"Weatherford, you don't mean—"

"Yes, *that* Weatherford." I breathed out a sigh. "You'll get your permission. It'll pass no one else's desk, but I need you to get her back."

## CHAPTER SIX

### Miranda

I whimpered as I felt the sting of the needle in my ass. I'm pretty sure the injection could have gone anywhere, but Danny liked me being on display. I'd never liked the way he looked at me, the touches that bordered on indecent.

His confession of watching me and Fate together still rang in my ears. I wasn't sure how he had seen us, but I knew *this* house had cameras in some rooms, although they lacked audio. John didn't take chances. He liked to know who was doing what and where. But they weren't everywhere, not when someone hacking the feed could be damning.

Every day John would drag me into the tiny bathroom. He'd lean against the wall, arms crossed, watching as Danny made me bend over, and place my hands on the fixed lid of the toilet tank, before he'd yank my panties down and jab me with whatever fertility drug it was he'd managed to get his hands on. I knew the lid was fixed because I'd tried to rip it off to hit him with it the first time he'd ran his hand over my ass, kneading it beneath his fingers. All part of the process, he'd say. He had to, because, for all the things that went on under this roof, John had never let anyone else touch me. I was his alone.

John didn't like Danny's hands on me. I could see the anger flash in his eyes every time he touched me. But the promise of a child was enough to still his temper, to ensure the combined clenching of his fist and jaw was the only repercussion.

Danny had been eager to start these injections. So much so, that after the first time John had finished proving he still wanted me, he'd sent for the doctor while his semen was still wet between my thighs. Apparently, the treatments had to start immediately. The blood work he'd taken on the ride back, to check I had stayed clean, had shown my hormones were exactly as they needed to be in order for optimum efficiency of this new drug. Although from the snippets of conversation I'd heard, I wondered if it had more to do with the large cash bonus he'd receive if I conceived.

A two-million-pound baby.

He never told me what the problem was with me, why I couldn't have children, but I prayed it was something no drug could fix. Because if he could deliver on his promise, if John planted his seed inside me, I'd have more than just myself to worry about. There would be the innocent life inside me that I'd need to protect from his wrath. I wasn't sure I was strong enough.

This was the seventh injection.

The seventh day I'd pretended to be his loving wife while my insides burned. I hated myself more every time I felt his hands upon me. My arm was raw from the times I had dragged my nails over the tattoo. I was ablaze. Burning. Spiralling. But he promised if I kept behaving, he'd let me leave the room soon.

I spent my days pacing, feeling the walls, counting them. One, two, three, four. Over and over in a loop as a distraction. I counted the paces from one side to another, reassuring myself the walls were not closing in, that there were still ten heel-to-toe paces between the bathroom's separating wall and the other side of the room.

I tried to keep myself busy. Think, solve problems in my mind. But sometimes it was all I could do to hold a coherent thought, and the small white room was driving me mad. So mad, that I actually started looking forward to the times I wasn't alone here, which only made my loathing grow.

It was a good job he'd removed the mirror because I didn't know how much more I could take. Especially since I now had a new roommate. My gaze sought the far corner of the room where the pet tarantula John had brought to keep me company sat, its hairy legs exploring the floor before it. Whenever he was with me, it got placed in a glass tank, but when he left, so too did the spider's prison. He knew these things terrified me. I spent all of last night not sleeping, my eyes fixed on it, always keeping as much distance between us as possible.

I felt my panties slide back into place, the final caress of my ass telling me he was done for another day.

"Same time tomorrow." Danny threw me a wink, my stomach churned in disgust. "I'll leave you two to have some fun." John's hand wrapped around my wrist, pulling me against him as he guided me back towards the mattress, eager to get on with business.

My gaze tore from the glass tank where the spider stood watching me, to the open door. It looked so bright out there, so fresh, so free. I just needed to be out there, just for a second. I didn't want to be here. I couldn't stand it. I just needed a second, something outside the white walls where the only disruption in the shade was from where my broken nails had clawed the paint from the brickwork.

Tears prickled behind my eyes, my chest rising and falling like a panicked animal. I needed out. I was barely surviving. If there was an off switch to life, I would have already pressed it a hundred times over.

Bastian stood guard in the doorway, waiting to escort Danny away. His dark hair had been gelled back, the slightest hint of motor oil on his cheek telling me it must be evening. The second his eyes met mine he dropped his gaze, no doubt hoping I wouldn't see the defeat.

He had nothing to feel guilty for. He'd kept his word; he hadn't told John where I'd ran. He needed to focus on his own family. His brother and sister were relying on him.

I tried to force my way to the door. I just needed to look outside, see the world beyond these walls. Just for a second, just a glimpse, then I would be a good girl again.

My stomach lurched as John tried to pull me back towards the mattress, away from the cool fragrance of fresh air that carried on the draught through the open door. But my feet wouldn't move.

"Please, John, please don't do this," I whimpered. I just needed to be out there. I couldn't stay here. Not again. Not another night alone with only madness and the largest spider I'd ever seen for company. I pulled back, his grip on my wrist crushing. "I've been good, please. It was a mistake. I only ran for you."

"Just a little longer, baby." He pushed his hand through my hair, his lips pressing against my cheeks, tasting my tears. "You can do that for me, right? I need to know you're here, you're safe. I was so damn scared when they found your car. You get that, don't you, baby. I need to know you're safe."

"I can be safe without you locking me up. Please."

"I missed you so much. Do you think I don't want you back in my bed? But you did this, Miranda. Not me. You."

"John, please."

"Just a little longer, baby." His arm swept beneath my legs, for a moment I thought he was letting me out. Hope blossomed in my chest as he carried me towards the door. Only to pull it closed. A sob caught in my throat as the catch engaged. "Come on, baby. I know you're upset, but I love you." My stomach burned with acid as he lay me on the mattress. I shoved him away from me. His hands wove in my hair until I felt the burn against my scalp as he drew my gaze to his. No. I needed to get out of here. "I love you so damn much. But if you're going to act like this, maybe I should go. I'll see you tomorrow." He released me from his grasp, rising to his feet.

My hand reached out to grab him before he had the chance to leave me alone in this quiet, dimly lit room. I didn't want to be alone. "Don't go." I hated that the words slipped from my lips. I saw him smile, the look of victory in his eyes. He knew he'd won.

I pulled his lips to mine. I couldn't be

alone. I fought the urge to bite his lip, to taste his blood. It was the first time I'd initiated anything between us, but I needed him to stay. I couldn't stand these walls anymore, and while he was here, the spider was trapped, like me, in its four tiny walls.

*Play nice and he'll let me out.* I kissed him back, pouring my desperation into it as my body quivered against his. But it wasn't anticipation, it was fear. I couldn't stay here. I'd do whatever I needed to. If he'd just let me out of this room, I'd be the woman he wanted me to be again. Anything.

"That's it, baby," he groaned, his fingers sliding down into my panties. He pushed me down to the mattress, smiling against my neck as his hot hungry kisses devoured me. I fought the urge to turn my head to the side like I had been doing.

I wanted him to think I wanted this, wanted him. I'd been good, let him do what he wanted. But it was clear he needed more, and I'd give him whatever it took if it meant getting out of this damn room. I closed my eyes with a whimper, wanting to ignore the hot breath against my skin, hoping he'd still mistake the quiet sounds I made as need rather than disgust.

His fingers traced the silk of the short nightgown he'd given me before he tugged it up, pushing aside my panties to plunge his fingers inside me. My nerves were ablaze. I hated that I was so raw, so desperate, that part of me acknowledged his touch felt good.

Play along.
Let it feel good.
Let go.

His fingers slid inside me, his thumb working tight, quick circles around my clit, and I moaned. John had never put this kind of effort in before I'd run. Before, only his own release had mattered. But Danny had told him making me orgasm increased the chances of a boy. He wanted a boy.

"I just need to know you're safe, baby," he whispered. "Come for me."

A sliver of fear chased across my skin. His touch felt good, but I was far from peaking. But I knew if I didn't at least fake it, he'd hurt me. It was important to him now. I focused on the sensation of his touch, my eyes tightly closed, moaning, imagining ocean blue eyes that still looked at me with love. I bucked and whimpered, tightening my muscles around his fingers, faking.

The cocky smile on his face told me I'd sold it. "Good girl." His hips lowered against me.

*Oh no. No, no, no.* I don't know why I fought mentally. It was destroying me. The first few times he'd fucked me I had screamed aloud. I knew better now.

I whimpered as he thrust inside me, his deep throaty moan bringing bile to my throat.

*Fake it.*

He thrust hard, his weight pressed upon me, hot, stifling, his hips swinging forward and back, hard enough to force the breath from my lungs as he fucked me into the mattress.

*Fake it.*

I moaned with each thrust, lifting my hips.

But then I wasn't faking any more. I felt the warmth coiling around my stomach, tightening, heating me from the inside out.
"That's it, baby."
The moans on my lips were no longer forced, they stemmed from the building heat, the sensation of friction. *Ocean blue eyes.* But this wasn't Fate. Fate hated me now. But his hate was justified. I knew that. He'd only known part of the story. I screwed my eyes closed tighter, but I could still hear John's moans, the sound of his testicles slapping against me with each vicious thrust.

My thighs ached, each thrust a heated ember adding to the building fire. "No. Oh God, no," I whimpered. Hating the heat chasing across my skin as I teetered on the edge of an orgasm. I realised too late I'd spoken aloud. He growled against me, his hand sliding around my throat. Panic seized me as he squeezed. My eyes bulged; fingernails clawed against his grip trying to pry him off.

I twisted and bucked, fighting for breath as he powered into me. He was getting off on my struggle, his fanatic grunts becoming more desperate as he choked the life from me.

Oh God, this was the end.

He'd been waiting, waiting for me to surrender, wanting one more ounce of humiliation, one more mind game.

The heat in my core continued to rise, burning, setting me aflame even as I fought to breathe. Light exploded behind my eyes, my body convulsed, confusing me as pleasure and fear mingled into one overwhelming sensation. How could I orgasm while fighting for my life? He slackened his grip, his release spilling into me like acid as I choked, dragging air into my lungs, unable to stop the vomit spilling from my mouth as I barely turned my head in time.

*You wanted this. This was your choice.* The voice in my mind mocked. I heard my nightie tear as he pulled me up, angry words echoing in my head that I couldn't quite make out. He pushed his hand through his hair, his furious gaze levelled at me.

"I-I'm sorry," I stuttered, my fingers rubbing my sore throat.

"Ungrateful bitch!" I felt myself strike the mattress, the taste of blood in my mouth from where my teeth bit my cheek. "Damn it, Miranda, why do you keep making me hurt you?" He clenched his fist, almost as if he was going to strike again before rising to his feet. I flinched as he dumped the spider onto the floor before the door slammed shut behind him.

I scurried to the door, pounding on it, sobbing my apologies. I had pretended with this man for eleven years. Why couldn't I be what he needed now, what was wrong with me?

He would parade me around his friends, I'd fake a smile, force a laugh, sell myself as the good wife. Be everything he needed. He trained me to be the perfect wife. I lived it for years. So why the hell couldn't I fake it now?

I needed to convince him, now more than ever. The white walls mocked me. My whole existence had narrowed just to him and the brief visit from Danny. A visit that reminded me there was a world outside these suffocating walls.

My gaze fixed on the pile of flowers in the corner of the room. One for every day I'd been here. Like me, they were slowly withering and dying. I watched the spider crawl up to them, claiming the only hint of colour in this room as its domain.

I pushed my back against the wall, wincing as my head fell against it. Pain. The pain felt good. It was something else. Something different. I leaned forward, bringing my head back again, slamming it against the solid wall with a loud thump. It hurt. But not enough, not enough to wipe out the fact his hands had been on me, the fact I had orgasmed, for real, felt my body react to him, for real.

I slammed my head back again, the force making me dizzy, the pain radiating through my skull all the way to my teeth. I needed to get out of here. There had to be a way. There had to be.

Think.

I slammed my head into the wall again.

Come on. Think.

## CHAPTER SEVEN

### Miranda

Twenty days. That's how long I'd been here. I knew because that's how many decaying flowers sat in the corner of the room.

My mind was a fog. I was being dragged around, back and forth from the bathroom to the mattress like a limp rag doll, barely able to function. I was doing everything John wanted. Everything. But he still wouldn't let me out of the room. He said it was for my own safety, that he was concerned for my health. If that were true, he wouldn't have left me in here.

I hadn't slept for four days. I'd been sleeping in John's arms until then, grateful for the feeling of comfort, for not being alone. But then, four days ago, I woke up to a soft caress on my arm, only it hadn't been John. John had left, leaving me alone with the spider.

I'd screamed bloody murder. The poor thing had dropped from my arm the moment I'd launched myself away, frantically putting distance between us while rubbing my arm where I swore I could still feel its tiny hairs. I was glad it ran off looking pissed off. While the things terrified me, I'd never hurt one.

Spiders were the only fear of mine John had ever seen. I'd quickly learnt my mistake. At first, it had been little things, like putting one in the bath or our room so he could come and save me. But once he tried his own version of exposure therapy. It didn't work. But he hadn't intended it to. I still had nightmares about that day. All those little black bodies.

One flower ago, Bastian had managed

to sneak to the door. It must have been late at night as he had told me the security team were applying an update to the security system software, so the cameras were off. He'd sat at the other side of the wooden barrier, talking to me. Telling me to hang in there, that he was working on something.

He told me to stay strong, and I had burst into tears.

I didn't have any strength left.

I was empty.

Broken.

He told me not to give up hope. But that only made things worse. Because there was no hope. Not anymore. Hearing his voice had been worse than the silence. It reminded me of the good times.

When Bastian first came to live in these walls, he hated me. I can't say I blamed him. I was the perfect accessory for John. I smiled, and laughed, showed him nothing but affection. I would sit on his lap, make loving eyes, and play make-believe. I was so good at pretending even John didn't know it wasn't real.

It didn't stop him hitting me though. It

only took him having a bad day, or my gaze lingering somewhere other than on him, and he made sure I remembered who the boss was.

On the outside, to those looking in we were happy. I was a doting wife. So why wouldn't Bastian hate me when he'd been forced to live under this roof after John had tracked him down, holding the life of his younger brother and sister hostage?

John insisted we spent time together and bonded. He was my brother-in-law. We were expected to be close as John believed there was no greater loyalty than the threads that bound family, specifically brothers. He had an odd way of showing it, but John was never sane in his expressions of love.

Bastian knew the rules, he knew the consequences, and so we played nice. While John was oblivious, seeing only what he wanted to, I could see the anger and hatred simmering in Bastian's eyes every time we were made to spend time together.

But after the incident in the shower, the fake show of protection, the make-believe brotherly affection that had once been laced with malice, became softer until, eventually, it was real.

The moments I had with him had felt like salvation. I'd almost forgotten what it was like not to pretend. One night, I trusted him enough to tell him the truth about Jenny hoping that if John took things too far with me, he could reach out and still protect his own family. I knew I was taking a big risk. It happened on the back of him discovering one of John's men had enrolled in the same classes as his little sister, for her protection, John insisted. But it was laced with threat, and we knew something big was going to happen if John felt the need to make such a bold move.

I promised him that when I eventually got away, it would be because the case was strong enough to take John down. His family would be safe. But that hadn't been the way things worked out.

It had been Bastian's idea for me to use the cover of the celebration to run. He'd spent a year, helping me draw out money in ways it wouldn't be seen, mainly by getting cash back on purchases John sent me to buy under discrete escort.

He kept the bag safe. When witness protection fell through, he used one of my tops to soak up the blood my husband spilt and told me how to fake my death so the absence of a body wouldn't even be questioned.

I'd had hope then. I'd known the case I helped build, with my testimony, would be enough to put John away. But now everyone thought I was dead. The accounts I'd handed off were useless without me to explain them.

As Bastian had sat outside the door, offering me assurances, I'd asked if he could get me something that would let me fall asleep and never wake up. He told me to hang in there.

Hang. In. There.

He didn't know what he was asking. The cramped room smelt of vomit. Hunger gnawed at my gut, but I could barely touch the food John was bringing me and, every time I moved my head, I felt like I was trapped on a carousel.

My eyes burned into the mattress. Where it touched the floor, I could see the underside was now worn, bobbled from the repeated friction of movement. I crawled towards it, a thought forming in my muddled mind.

Tipping the mattress, I could see the outlines of the springs straining against the fabric. A scratch, scored into the varnished wooden floor, sent a flurry of excitement through me. Flipping the mattress, I found the small spike of a penetrating coil. It sank into my thumb as I grasped at it, twisting rotating, drawing it through the fabric until it was in my hand.

I toyed with it, pressing it against the pad of my thumb where its sharp edge had drawn a single drop of blood. I imagined thrusting it into John's throat, but I knew that was no good. I wouldn't be able to inflict the damage I needed to escape. Unless ...

Crawling to the corner, until my back pressed against the wall, I looked at my arm. I couldn't do enough damage to John to escape him, but maybe I could still escape.

    I studied my arm through tired blurred eyes, looking for the thickest blue line. I clenched my jaw, nodding to myself, giving permission, steeling myself before digging the spring deep into my arm. Pain lanced through me, my teeth gritted so hard I thought they would break as I forced myself to breathe slowly through my nose, dragging the edge of the spring upwards. There was blood, but not enough. Deeper. I needed it to be deeper. My entire body trembled as I pressed harder, digging the metal deeper until I felt the slow trickle of blood down my arm increase.

    I watched the vibrant red fluid with morbid fascination, a laugh on my lips as I grew light-headed. A moment of panic passed quickly, embraced, and released as I accepted what I'd done. I wasn't giving up. I just wasn't letting him win.

    I closed my eyes, imagining the ocean blue eyes I loved, summoning his presence to my mind. I pretended I could feel the warmth of his hand in mine, allowed myself the lie of one long, slow goodbye filled with all the painful, churning, unending love I had for Fate.

As much as his words had broken me, he'd also been one of the few people to build me up. His goodness, my love for him, far outweighed the pain of a few words spoken in anger. I saw that now, I'd recognised it days ago as I stood clawing the walls, screaming vows and promises mingled with bitterness. I would have said anything, done anything if John would have let me out of these walls. Just as Fate had said anything in the heat of his rage.

He'd had every right to be angry, feel betrayed. I should have fought harder to stay and make him listen. I should have told him everything. My failings were not his to shoulder. The mocking voice in my head was not his to hear.

Jesse Fateson deserved better than a beaten down, worthless, addict, but I was grateful for every minute he had spent showing me what it was to truly be loved. For one moment I had known what it felt like not to be wretched, but to be lifted by his presence and feel something glorious. I was like Icarus, and Fate was the sun. I'd flown too close, but the fall was worth it to bask in his presence for even a second.

My mind fought to settle on the single most prolific memory to carry me into the darkness. But the thing about Fate was, every second with him had been a slice of heaven. I had never been so whole and loved than when I stood beside him basking in his glory, watching him shine with radiance. He was my sun, my world revolved around him. But now my star was dying, and I just wanted one more look at the light before darkness wrapped me in its cold embrace. One last breath I could pretend to share with him.

The ghost of a kiss on my lips dissipated as the sound of hurried footsteps echoed down the silent hallway outside. The fumbling of the key in the lock fixed to the bolt sounded distance. I should have barricaded the mattress against the door to buy me a minute or two. I should have remembered there were cameras here. For a moment, as the door flew open to reveal John, refreshing the stagnant tang of vomit with fresh crisp air, it was like watching him in slow motion. His face was a mask of frustration, but then the disbelief washed over him as his eyes followed the flow of the crimson fluid. He moved in a flash, yanking the metal spring from my grasp, his hand clamping over my wrist.

"What did you do?" he growled. His fingers becoming slick with blood. I felt my lips curl into a tired smile, heard the echo of my high-pitched laughter as I watched him, darkness edging my vision. "What the fuck did you do?"

Rolling my head, my gaze fixed on the door, and I inhaled deeply. It was open.

"Doctor Tavott!" I heard Bastian's voice break as he appeared in the doorway, hollering for the doctor. The sound of running. John was pushed aside; voices swam in my mind.

"If anything happens to the baby, it'll be your head, am I making myself clear?" John threatened.

*Baby?*

My free hand dropped to my stomach involuntarily.

No. I couldn't be pregnant.

What had I done?

"Stay with me, baby." John's hands were in my hair, stroking me desperately, I could feel the sticky trail of fluid transferred from his hands, his gaze flitting between me and Danny.

"It's not deep, looks worse than it is."

"And the baby?"

"I'd have to get her to hospital. We don't have the equipment here."

The sound of splintering wood from downstairs made John stiffen. He released me. "Bastian, watch her," he barked. Something was happening. I could hear yelling, shouting from somewhere far away. Danny stepped away, fleeing the room on John's heels.

I felt myself being pulled onto Bastian's lap, his strong arms encircling me, his lips on my head as he rocked me gently. "Mira, I'm so sorry." I could feel the dampness from his cheeks as he buried his face in my hair, rocking me back and forth as I drifted to sleep. "I'm so fucking sorry."

## CHAPTER EIGHT

### Miranda

Bastian stayed with me when the paramedics took me away. He never left my bedside. His jaw tight, eyes burning as the doctors and nurses came in and out of the private room. A police officer had been posted outside my door, but no one would tell me why. No one would tell me anything.

I didn't recognise the doctor who was looking at me, but I could see the judgement in her eyes. Who was she to judge me? She had no idea what I'd been through. She had no idea what had driven me to this.

The woman spent more time looking at the notes on her tablet than at me. Telling me the wound hadn't been deep or serious. It had felt both. My grasp tightened on Bastian's hand as she confirmed I was pregnant, before mentioning something about a psychiatric evaluation before leaving the room. As the door closed behind her I stiffened. Trying not to focus on the fact my world was once again reduced to four sealed walls. I needed to think about something else.

I was pregnant.

My free hand rested on my stomach as I searched inside myself. I'm not sure what I was meant to be feeling, but I was numb. Even though I knew there was a life growing inside me, a miracle baby I thought I'd never have, a child who would be loved and wanted regardless of where it came from, my gaze kept returning to the closed door. I kept seeing that seal. The way the door sat flush against the wall, muting the sounds of the ward outside.

While the slats on the windows had been opened, the restriction burning across my chest wouldn't ease. "I need to get out of here," I whispered. The walls may have changed, but I was still trapped. There was no way to get through that window, it was designed to stop people from doing the very thing I wanted to.

"We need to wait for the police. We don't know—" He glanced away.

"You know something."

"Yes. But I think it's best you wai—"

"Tell me."

"Jenny turned up at the garage. I'd been trying to get in contact with her without raising suspicion. I needed to let her know you were alive. But the number had been disconnected. Last week, she pulled her car into my shop, claiming there was an issue with the motor, and broke down in tears.

"I took her to the back. The minute we're out of sight, the tears stop, like switching off a faucet, and she asks if I've seen you. Apparently, they exhumed the remains and found out it wasn't you in the coffin."

"I don't understand."

"Someone tipped them off you were alive. NCA need your testimony, so they issued a warrant for Avery's arrest and a recovery team. They were meant to arrest everyone in the property but ..."

"But?"

"John and Doctor Tavott weren't amongst the arrests."

My pulse quickened. My hand dropping to my stomach protectively as his fingers intertwined with mine. "I imagine Doctor Tavott took the money and ran." His gaze lifted; his brown eyes filled with sympathy. "I'm sorry. I tried everything to get to you. But John wanted to handle you personally. He wanted the only contact you had to be him. How are you feeling?" His gaze dropped to the dressing on my arm, regret flooding his features.

I could hear every question he wasn't asking. He'd seen the state of that room, the claw marks chipping the white paint, the mattress left on the polished floor. He'd smelt the vomit and met my

# SAVING GRACE

roommate. He knew how much John enjoyed his mind games, the perverse pleasure he gained from them. I probably should have been feeling more, but there was an emptiness inside me, and the only thoughts racing through my mind were, I needed to get out of here, and thank God I wasn't alone.

The silence in that room had been deafening. I'd never known tarantulas hissed. How loud they were. My hands rubbed up and down my arms, trying to shake away the imaginary feeling of its legs upon me. When I didn't answer he scooted me along on the bed, crawling in beside me to take me in his arms. The way he pulled me against his chest, offering me warmth and contact, was all the permission I'd needed to finally fall apart.

"Tell me what you need. Anything. I'll make it happen."

There was only one answer. One thing I needed, but he didn't need me.

Fate.

So maybe I could have the next best thing. He may have said there was no place for me there but—"I want to go home."

## Miranda

I don't think any of what Jenny said to me sank in. Bastian had only left my side to bring me snacks. He made me smile, sniffing at the hospital food like it was poison. I know hospital food has a bad rep, but this stuff was pretty damn good, it would have been even better if I could have kept it down. Of course, the burger and fries he'd brought me had been even better, but even with a will of iron, it still joined the rest of the food, spiralling down the white ceramic toilet as I puked my guts out until my chest and stomach hurt from the strain.

While Jenny was talking, all I was doing was closing my eyes, imagining the sound of the waves against the shore. Pretending I wasn't trapped in another small room with no way out. I'd been here a day, so long as I wasn't alone it was bearable but, at times, I still needed to remind myself I wasn't in the white room, because sometimes, as I fought with fatigue and nausea, it was difficult to remember exactly where I was.

"Are you listening?" Jenny pushed her honey blonde hair behind her ears. It had been up in a high ponytail when she'd first walked into the room. I must have been stressing her out because at some point she'd tugged it free. She looked like one of those women from a hair product commercial. Even though her hair had been up, it now fell to her shoulders in beautiful curls, as if she'd just stepped foot from the hairdressers. She chewed the arm of her glasses, her deep brown eyes studying me. Waiting for my answer.

What had she been saying? Something about ... oh I don't know. I can't even pretend I was paying attention. She sighed indulgently. It didn't help she was talking so quietly. Everyone here still thought she was just my sponsor, even the cop at the door.

"Okay, I know you've gone through a shock, but I need to know what you want to do. John is still out there. We can move you to a safe house until—"

"No!" My pulse spiked, sending the

monitors attached to me racing, causing the digital lines to spike vigorously. I was *not* going to leave one prison only to find myself in another. I needed to be outside, feel the wind on my face, smell the sea air, inhale the fragrance of lavender and vanilla mingled with the musky scent of—*Stop it!* I need to stop torturing myself. Fate doesn't want me. He never will. But I can still have everything else. I hope.

Even if I found a way to make him listen to my side of the story, told him I wasn't married, that I'd been running, explained everything, there was one damning fact I couldn't hide. I was carrying another man's child.

He'd already told me I was just like his ex-wife, the woman who'd cheated on him and had his best friend's baby. I was her carbon copy now, right down to the other man's baby. Even if he could forgive me for the secrets, there was no way he could look past this. Maybe, though, I could still build a home and a life in Barrett's Bay.

While I was trapped in the white room, I'd had a lot of time to think. I forced myself to understand that the words Fate had spoken had come from a place of hurt. That his words, while they tore me apart, had been formed from incomplete facts. I only had myself to blame. I should have just told him the truth from the start.

"We need to keep you safe." Jenny's soft whisper pulled me from my thoughts.

"I need to go home." That's exactly what I needed to do, especially if John was still out there somewhere. He'd drilled into me what had to happen should a raid ever be made on our home. He didn't believe they would ever uncover anything to warrant an arrest, but he had a plan in place. I had to be seen to be following orders, especially if I wanted to keep everyone safe.

My hand stroked my stomach gently.

I was going to keep everyone safe.

I knew how his mind worked. He'd already know I was here, and if I didn't follow the plan, he'd hurt Bastian's siblings, for no other reason than, the moment he'd fled and left me with his half-brother, Bastian was expected to keep me safe, away from the cops, and ensure I did as was expected.

"You can't go back to John's. We don't know where he is but—"

John's? That place wasn't my home. Besides my plan was better. John knew I'd passed through Barrett's Bay thanks to the police check. If he looked up the place, he'd have seen it was quiet, remote, the exact kind of place he'd expect me to hide. He wouldn't risk going there himself. We'd been separated, which meant we had to stay that way. Right now, I needed to hide away, and prove my loyalty to him by following his contingency plan. If I didn't, if he got the faintest hint of anything amiss, it wouldn't just be my life in danger. No-one turned traitor against John.

"I want to go back to—"

"They found you there once," Bastian interrupted. His voice was nothing more than a low whisper in my ear as he shifted on the bed beside me.

"Danny found me there, but—" I wondered if Danny had kept his word. He had promised that if I left willingly, he'd tell

John the detective there only ran my name because I passed through the town looking like death. I'd heard him tell John about tracking me across the country, finding me in the room of a seedy motel. I had to believe he'd kept his word. Besides, Danny would have run. He was careful. All the work he did for John was on contract. He got paid generously for his work, but he made sure it was all above board. He would have taken his cash bonus and disappeared. I'd be surprised if he hadn't returned home, back to New York.

"We need to put you in a safe house," Jenny stressed quietly.

Safe house was just another word for prison. "I can't do it, Jenny. I won't be confined." I dropped my head looking to my hands, shifting uncomfortably on the hospital mattress that seemed to reflect every ounce of heat back at me to an uncomfortable degree. I shifted again, making the bed creak. It was nearly impossible to get comfortable on these things, even with the head raised, and all the pillows behind me I didn't feel I was sitting properly. "Besides, if one person finds out who shouldn't ..." I shook my head, leaving the sentence hanging.

"Look," she raised her voice a little, enough to make me flinch, but still be unheard outside. "If you're telling me you refuse to testify unless I let you stay wherever the hell you want, then you're not leaving me a choice." *Thank you, Jenny.* "But, there's going to be conditions."

"Okay. However," I looked to Bastian. "I'm willing to document everything, give you every detail, every name, but I need assurances." She didn't know the file already existed. When I first went to work for Doc I'd stashed a binder in with some ancient invoices, hiding it perfectly where no-one would think to look.

It had been my back up. A way to make sure Bastian and his siblings were safe and John was taken down, even if something happened to me. I hadn't thought it through though, because whilst I had hidden it, I hadn't told a single person of its existence. By the time I realised my oversight, it was too late. It had just become a useless, forgotten file, gathering dust.

"We can keep you safe. You'll have a new name, bank accounts, a whole new identity."

"No. We do this my way. I want a detail placed on Bastian's siblings until this is over." I felt Bastian's arms stiffen around me. He needed people following Jake and Rosie, John needed to think the police were looking for him if my plan was going to work, and I needed to know they would be safe.

"We've negotiated that as part of his test—"

"Oh no. He's not testifying." Not a chance in hell. The moment he got up on the stand, he'd be dead, but not before they made him watch his siblings suffer. No, he was not getting near this. This didn't touch him. John had to believe he was one hundred percent loyal. "And as far as anyone is concerned, except yourself, they're being placed under surveillance in case Bastian tries to make contact."

"But we—"

"I'm not negotiating. You promised me

four years ago I'd get witness protection. If you'd pulled me out sooner, Bastian and his family wouldn't have been dragged into this." A lie, but she had no idea how deep and how far this thing reached, and I'd protected everyone, especially Bastian. "You kept me there because you realised this was bigger than you thought. You owe me this. You owe him—" There it was, the fire inside me I thought had extinguished. I felt it slowly rekindle inside me as the need to protect those I cared for surfaced. I had to be strong now, I had to do this right. Because it wasn't only me at risk. He wasn't going to hurt anyone I cared for, not again.

"Mira, it's okay, re—"

"No." I blinked back some tears. Why was I crying? I was feeling empowered, strong, determined. I cupped my hand over my mouth, trying to compose myself. Was it too early for my hormones to be running amuck? I thought about all the stories Bastian had told me about his family, Rosie, his sister, was twenty-one now, his brother, Jake, was twenty-four, and he'd been their legal guardian since their stepfather died when Bastian was nineteen. That was one of the reasons he'd started work as a mechanic in the first place. And John, the moment Mr Avery died, dragged Bastian deeper into the twisted empire he had built.

If John even suspected Bastian had turned on him, there wasn't a thing that could be done to protect him or his family. He needed to be seen as keeping silent, staying loyal as he was expected to do. It was the only way he'd keep his family safe. Since Bastian had been charged with looking after me, John would think he was still on his side, so long as nothing the NCA did compromised that. I twisted, cupping his hand in my face. "I need you safe." I glanced around, making sure no one but the people in the room could hear me. "There's nothing to tie Bastian to anything."

"They used his body shop," Jenny began.

"And paid off the employees there to do work under the table. There's not a thing you can hold over his head. I should know." Yeah, I knew alright, because even though he'd hated me, I'd made sure not a trace of anything illegal could fall back on him. He may not have recognised that I was there under duress at first, but it didn't mean I had been blind. I'd also let John know what I was doing, saying I did it under the guise of ensuring nothing ever reached his brother, which would allow him to open further franchises without raising any flags, even if his original shop was ever discovered to be shady.

"Mira, what are you—"

"As far as the accounts show, they used your garage without your knowledge, and they can't prove otherwise. John trusts you, he'll expect you to say and do whatever it takes to stay by my side and keep your niece or nephew safe." My voice cracked again. "I know how his mind works. He thinks family are bound with loyalty. He won't believe I've turned on him, and he'll think you're protecting me."

"What are you saying?"

"I'm saying, if you slap us in witness protection, or hide us away in a safe house now, we're as good as dead. But if you let me go, he'll think me and Bastian are lying low. Following orders." Ever since that scare eleven months ago we had been given a plan of action.

"Miranda, do you know where he is?"

I shook my head. But even if I had I wouldn't have dared tell her.

## CHAPTER NINE

### Jesse

Relief. That was the only way to describe what I was feeling right now. Pure, unadulterated, fucking relief. I don't think my heart knew what to do now my chest had managed to expand, drawing in the sweetest breath of air I'd ever tasted, knowing she was not only alive but safe.

I hadn't been given details, only that a team had entered the property yesterday and extracted her using information obtained from someone Jenny knew inside the house. She hadn't known anything more until someone in the hospital rang the I.C.E—In Case of Emergency—number on file. Jenny had ensured she was listed years ago, detailed as her sponsor. There was a flag on the file her team had put on several months back, so even if Grace was accompanied to the hospital, they still rang the number on file. She'd known Grace was safe since yesterday, and I was more than a little pissed off she hadn't rung me to tell me until now, more so when she told me to stay put. Like that was even an option.

My hands tightened around the steering wheel as my heart fluttered. The world seemed lighter, brighter for knowing she was still here. I had a hundred things I wanted to say, a thousand promises. A plan. I was going to walk into that hospital, take her in my arms, and beg her to forgive me. I was going to win her back. I hurt her, hurt myself with how I'd treated her. But I was determined to fix it. I would spend every day for the rest of my life showing her she was everything, showing her she wasn't worthless but beyond value.

Jenny didn't say much about her condition when the call came through. I didn't ask about the baby; I don't even know if she knew. It wasn't that I didn't care, but Grace was my priority. I had to make sure she was okay. Anything else came after. She had been left with that monster nearly three weeks, and it was three weeks too long. Three weeks that could have been avoided if only I'd have used my brain instead of assuming the worst.

Guilt and anger knotted my stomach. Whatever she'd been made to suffer was on me. Would she even be able to look at me? I was asking the impossible. She'd stood at the doctor's surgery door, begging for a chance to explain, and I wouldn't give her one. It'd serve me right if she spat in my face. My words hadn't only hurt her, they'd put her life in danger. I don't know that I'd ever be able to express how truly sorry I was. I didn't deserve a second chance. But I was damn well going to fight for one, fight for her.

I was not too proud to beg. I'd get on my knees if I had to. Hell, I'd crawl naked over glass if that's what it took.

I slipped into the store in the hospital lobby just inside the main entrance, carefully selecting several types of chocolate, listening to the excited chatter of the store clerks. Then, just as the lady rang my order up, she cast me a glance, her eyes twinkling in the kind of delight I saw reflected in Dotty's gaze when she was imparting the latest gossip.

"It's awful, isn't it?" It took me a second to realise she was now addressing me instead of the lady who'd just left. She was an older woman, mid-fifties, with a sparkle of mischief in her eyes. Yes, this woman was definitely the hospital's version of Dotty. No doubt about it. I looked in the direction she inclined her head, to see a uniformed officer joining the queue at the coffee shop. "Haven't you heard? Ooh, it's just terrible. Someone sneaked out from under armed guard. Well not armed, per se, but you know what I mean. They've got the hospital in a right tizzy." I probably

would have fixated on the word tizzy, if not for the implication, but my gut was already churning. Foreboding washed over me with its sickly-sweet heat.
"Do you know who?"
"Some suicide watch from last night. From what I heard, she came in with a police escort. Caused quite the fuss too, since everyone thought she was dead. It's been all over the news."
My hand grasped the counter, suicide watch? Missing? It took me a moment to realise the clerk was watching me expectantly. Grabbing the chocolates, I tossed some notes on the counter, my legs feeling oddly unstable as I left the store, ignoring her call about my change. My vision scanned the boards looking for the ward. There was no way I heard that right. There had to be some mistake.
My mind didn't even know what to focus on, the fact if the pit in my stomach was right, Grace had tried to end her life, or the fact she was missing. I don't know which blow hit the hardest. I tried to breathe through the familiar constriction.

# SAVING GRACE

There was nothing certain, it wasn't necessarily Grace. It would be someone else. I'd get to the room, and she'd be there. Waiting. Safe. Yeah, I just needed to keep telling myself that.

Each echo of my boots on the tiled floor pounded in time with the rapid beat of my heart. Making my way towards the ward and room number I'd been given; I noticed the increase in police presence. It was a second later I caught sight of Jenny inside a side room, being drilled by some uniforms.

Sliding up to the nurses' station, I lingered nearby as if waiting for someone. The cops who saw me weren't interested. I looked just like any other visitor.

Through the open door, I could hear their low conversation.

"No, officer. I got a call from the hospital yesterday to say she'd been admitted. I'm her sponsor," Jenny explained, her voice quivering with grief. "I thought she was dead ... I—" she sniffled, accepting the tissue from the cop. Wow, she was really good. "I thought I'd failed her. They told me she'd overdosed. I went to her funeral." Jenny pulled her glasses off, wiping the tear misted glass on her cardigan, taking the chance to lift her vulnerable shimmering eyes to the officer asking the questions. I take back every doubt I had about her ability.

"Was anyone else with her when you left?"

"Only Sebastian, that's John's brother."

*What?* I couldn't have just heard that right.

"He wouldn't leave her side. I figured it was okay since John wasn't here himself. I'm not sure why they had someone outside the door. I didn't think that was normal, but I guess it makes sense since she was on suicide watch."

I listened as the police explained John was a person of interest in a case. Jenny acted the role perfectly. I remembered how easily such things had come to me back in the day as well. Although my undercover stint had only lasted eight months, I still remembered how hard we trained to erase our tells.

I'd heard all I needed to. Leaving the chocolates at the nurses' station, I slipped from the hospital, sliding into the car. Jenny's words echoing around my mind.

Suicide watch. What that shopkeeper said had been right.

Had Grace really tried to take her own life? I rested my head against the steering wheel. This was all my fault. I had to find her. Jenny said she was admitted with Avery's brother, he had to have done something to her. He'd probably waited for a quiet moment and dragged her from safety. Maybe he'd taken her to wherever Avery was hiding. I slapped the wheel, frustration coiling my every muscle.

Shit.

What did I do now?

The passenger door opening caused me to jolt. Slipping an Uber sign on my windscreen Jenny slid beside me. "Drive."

I did as instructed, my trembling hands stabbing the key toward the ignition several times before it finally drove home. "What's going on? Where's Grace?" I asked as I pulled from the hospital car park, checking my mirrors to make sure no one was following us.

"Grace?"

"Miranda, where is she?"

"Things didn't go quite as planned."

"No kidding. What the fuck had the officers been thinking, leaving her with the brother of a man with a warrant out for his arrest?"

"Bastian's clean."

"No one around Avery is clean." My hands tightened on the wheel. "You know something. Where. Is. She?" I ground out.

"I don't know where she is, but I know where she'll be. That's why I told you to stay put." She sighed. "There is something you need to know, in case something happens to me." She pulled a paper from somewhere inside her top, sliding it into my glove box. I caught the slightest glimpse of the stamp and realised it was something to do with Grace. Something meant to protect her. Whatever agreement she and Grace had reached was on that paper. "Mira said if she was forced into witness protection Avery would know she'd turned and ensure she never made it to testify."

"Turned? You say that as if she had a choice in anything she did," I bristled, taking a corner a little too hard, sending her jerking towards the passenger door roughly.

Instead of responding, she continued as if I'd never spoken. "Her best option was to disappear. Sebastian is responsible for watching her when John isn't around, so they decided to flee the hospital and follow protocol. She's heading to Barrett's Bay. Avery would expect them to find somewhere to lie low, and since he thinks she stopped by there on the way—"

"Wait, stopped by?"

"Apparently, Doctor Tavott struck a deal with her. She went back, and he'd tell Avery the cop in town only ran a background check because she passed through the town looking questionable." She levelled a glare at me over her glasses, as if I didn't already know I'd fucked up by doing that. "In return, he'd make sure Avery didn't know about you, and the people she'd been close to there. She needs to act like she's still on his side."

"You're sure she'd heading to Barrett's Bay?"

"Yes. With a warrant for his arrest, Avery won't follow her there. He'll lie low and find a way to get word to Bastian for a rendezvous. Turn left here," Jenny instructed. "The details are in there, fax it to Weatherford and get it on his record. This remains between us three until John's in custody. We can't afford a leak."

"She's definitely coming home?" I was dubious. Grace was with Avery's fucking brother. He couldn't be trusted. Abuse victims often found a reason to side with their abuser.

I don't know what the fucker put her through that made her feel like she'd had no choice but to try to take her own life, but I was willing to bet this Sebastian character was as rotten as his brother. Every minute she was alone with him she was in danger. Hell, he could have taken her straight back to Avery, it's not like she'd be in a condition to resist. Jenny had to know there was a chance Grace had only been placating her.

    Jenny nodded. "I'm sure. I can't have anyone posted there. I have to assume he'll get eyes on her sooner rather than later, and it would look too suspicious if a quiet town suddenly has an influx of fresh faces. For obvious reasons, we're the only ones who know the break from the hospital was planned." She patted the glove box again. Now I understood why she'd documented it. Grace running would likely be spun as a sign of guilt. Jenny didn't know who to trust either.

    "I'll keep her safe." *If* she turns up, because right now I wasn't betting on it.

    "Good. I was hoping you'd say that."

## Miranda

It had been three days since we left the hospital. We sneaked out in the morning when the guard had a sudden desperate urge to visit the bathroom after drinking the coffee Bastian had bought him. From there, he boosted a car and drove. Leaving it in a car park. We changed vehicles twice more. Sleeping in the car and often driving late into the night before finding a lay-by or service station to rest in.

Even though I could drive, he refused to let me behind the wheel. To be honest, after my last experience driving, I was quietly grateful. Eventually, as we neared the outskirts of some city centre, the petrol tank spluttered, and we rolled to a stop at the side of a busy city road. Leaving the hazards on, we walked to the closest supermarket, where we got a change of clothes and the first hot meal we'd had.

I would like to have said my stomach relished the hot food, that I had more luck keeping the full English breakfast down than the pre-made sandwiches and salads, but all I ended up doing was nibbling the corners of the toast and emptying my stomach.

Bastian used his credit card at every opportunity. In the city, we went to the bank, drew out a load of cash, and used it to buy a second-hand car we'd seen on the supermarket lot. The owner had been all too happy to instantly part with his eight-hundred-pound ride for a grand, he even let Bastian use his phone to register the tax. Things were so much easier when the tax was transferable between car owners.

With a new car, and the transfer of ownership papers posted, we stocked up on supplies and began our journey, doubling back down quiet roads and sleeping in the car.

Jenny would be cross. I had promised we'd go straight to our destination, but with the trail we'd left, it would send anyone looking for us this way, while we ran the other. It was what John would have expected us to do. Stick to the plan and no one gets hurt.

I closed my eyes, letting the air from the cracked window wash over me, pushing back the tides of nausea that seemed to ebb and flow. My stomach was trapped in perpetual motion, and the uneven country roads hadn't helped one bit.

I guess this is what people meant by morning sickness, but I knew something for certain, they'd got the name wrong. It should have been all the damn time sickness. I'd done nothing but feel like I wanted to puke my guts out since discovering I was pregnant. Hell, I'd been vomiting even before that. I just hadn't realised it was because Danny's treatments had been successful. I'd flipped between it being my body's reaction to John touching me and a side effect of the fertility drug.

Bastian glanced over to me, clearing his throat. I dropped my hand, pretending I hadn't been scratching my arm raw. I clenched the loose fabric of the trousers we'd picked up, giving my fingers something else to do as my mind homed in on a single, Earth-moving thought.

I was going to be a mother.

When Danny had told me I couldn't have children, it'd felt as though the rug had been pulled out from under me. Yes, I'd had my suspicions something was wrong. You couldn't try for a baby for four years without success, and not have some doubts, but hearing him say those words had hurt, more than how John had beaten me.

I mourned the child I would never

have. I had always envisioned having a family, but I had never wanted John to be a father. I stroked my stomach. It didn't matter who the sperm donor had been, countless women got inseminated having never met the man. This was my baby, and he or she would grow up knowing only love. They wouldn't be raised like me, wouldn't be made to feel worthless.

All my life I had wanted to feel important to someone, like I was enough, well, this baby would be my priority. They would never doubt my love. Not for one second. And selfishly, I knew deep down, being the centre of this little person's world, being enough for them, was more than I could have asked for.

"You doing okay?"

"Yeah," I answered on instinct, too quickly. But was I? The roads had turned familiar now, even the amber-tinted light, that warned twilight was just a few hours away, felt different here. I recognised the trees, the way they stretched out over the country roads.

When I was young, on the bus, I used

to pretend this archway was the portal to a magical kingdom. The moment I passed the trees, it always felt like a weight had been lifted. This was my place of transition; the moment I stopped being Miranda, the unwanted child who could never measure up against her brilliant sister, and became someone else, someone who knew love and friendship.

My body knew to relax by instinct when I passed under these trees, but this time, the tension just coiled, growing tighter.

*There's no place for someone like you here.'*

I pushed the voice from my mind, the pain from my chest. I didn't need Jesse Fateson to tell me I wasn't welcome in my own home. I'd just avoid him. My world may have revolved around him, but I would find a way to change course. He was the bright sun who had been my salvation, but I would no longer be a star in his orbit. Broken planets didn't survive, they drifted like a comet, hurtling through space and, with any luck, our paths would not pass for a long time, because I knew the moment I was near him, it would take everything I had not to be caught in his gravitational field again.

"Talk to me." Bastian pulled into a passing place on the side of the road. I focused on the traditional style wooden farm gate, noticing the heavy metal chains and padlocks preventing people from venturing onto the farmer's land. I let myself stare absentmindedly, pretending I hadn't heard the plea in his voice. I wasn't ready for this conversation. He placed his hand on my thigh, giving it a reassuring squeeze. "I'm not moving the car until you talk to me. Something's going on, something happened here. I saw it on your face when Tavott brought you back." When I didn't answer, he twisted in his seat, reaching through to the back, pulling something from his backpack. "I have candy." He added a teasing lilt to his voice, waving the chocolate in front of me. I moved to snatch it, but he pulled it away.

"You'd really deny your future niece or nephew food?" He froze for a moment, moving quickly before I managed to swipe it. "It's nothing to worry about," Not a lie, he didn't have any cause for concern.

"You're forgetting who you're talking to."

"Fine," I huffed, crossing my arms. "There was a guy." I hate my voice quivered, how I couldn't bring myself to speak his name aloud.

"You were close?"

I nodded, tears spilling from my eyes. I wasn't just close to him though. I loved him. He was the first person I had ever wanted to give those words to. The heel of my hand massaged my chest as if it could rub away the ever-present ache. I didn't want to love him. I just couldn't help it. Telling my soul not to yearn for him was like trying to tell my lungs not to breathe, my heart not to beat. It was a reflex, instinctive, essential to survival.

But just because I felt this way, it didn't mean it had to consume my every thought. I didn't have to think about my organs for them to work, they just did. And so, I would bury my love for him as deep as I could until, eventually, it became nothing more than a dull ache in my soul. Barely present, but always there.

My feelings for him had given his words the power to tear me apart, confirming every single thing I always feared about myself. He broke my heart, shattering it into a million splinters. But it still beat for him, driving the splintered remains deep into my soul, embedding themselves in such a way I knew I'd never truly be rid of them.

"Then why do you look like someone just killed your puppy?"

I took a deep breath, forcing my voice through the emotions as I told him about the last time I had seen Fate. The way I'd panicked after he'd discovered my fake IDs and the cash, how I'd run, only to discover he was a cop. I explained how I had planned to tell him everything, my fears about doing so and how, before I had a chance, he discovered the truth for himself and in a flash anything I thought he had felt for me turned to hate. He'd made it clear I would never be welcome in

Barrett's Bay.

Bastian held me, his tall frame twisted across the gearstick awkwardly as he pulled me close and let me cry. It felt good to finally let it all out. To say his name aloud.

"Want me to kill him?" Bastian asked softly as he held me. I shook my head, forcing a laugh through the tears. With his black hair, dark eyes, muscular physique, and some of his mother's subtle Italian features, he looked dangerous when he wanted to, but there was no denying, the man was more of a brooding Casanova than the Godfather. The only time I'd ever seen him raise his hand to anyone, was when one of John's guests thought that me being the only female in the house meant I attended to *all* the guests' needs.

I shudder to think what could have happened if Bastian hadn't been there. Normally the men John invited into his home knew their place. But this had been different. He'd arrived while John was away. Word had been sent to Jeeves to get everything in place, but the man had no idea of etiquette. The moment he was patched up he'd cornered me in the kitchen, taking my legs out from under me and fisted my hair in his hands as he fumbled with his zipper.

He'd needed Danny's services again after Bastian was finished with him. But instead of allowing him to see the doctor, the man had been kicked to the curb. It was the only time I'd ever seen Bastian lose his temper. He'd driven his fists into the man with fierce precision. Shattering his nose, cheekbone, and who knew what else.

Then, with his fists still covered in the man's blood, he'd held me in his arms, checked I was okay, and did the damnedest thing, he'd fixed me a bowl of ice cream at the kitchen counter, and stood behind me, brushing the knots from my hair, until every sense of that man's touch had been removed.

It was one of the rare times Bastian had looked after me so tenderly while in the full view of the cameras. John had approved of how he'd protected me the way a brother should, although there had still been a glimmer of something jealous in his eyes, knowing that another man, even his brother, had touched me with such tenderness.

"No," I whispered finally, as my strength slowly returned. He held me a moment longer until my shuddering breathing calmed.

"Here." He passed me the promised chocolate. "Be sure to point him out, I'll make sure he doesn't get in spitting distance. Are you sure this is where you want to be? There's plenty of other small towns."

"I'm sure." He turned the car over again and began driving. Before he could pull into town, I stopped him, guiding him towards the separate garages.

Barrett's Bay was a tiny forgotten town overlooking a beautiful cove. The roads were narrow seeing very little in the way of traffic, and the pavements had an old-fashioned charm, perfectly cobbled. One year, when I was young, the council had wanted to fill in the cobbles with tarmac where some had been dislodged. Before they could ruin the rustic streets, the vicar had gathered a few locals, and together they'd reset the cobbles back to their glory, saying once the council began ripping things up, they never ended up the same again.

Walking the streets, seeing the old cast-iron style streetlights, it often felt like taking a step back in time. Several houses had their own garages, but for those that didn't, there was a large section of land just outside the town with garages, one for each property. I hadn't given much thought to them last time I'd been here. I'd lost my car in the crash, and to be fair, I didn't even remember arriving here as such.

I slipped out of the car; the gravel crunched beneath my feet as I worked my way across to Gramps' garage. My fingers traced across the empty eyeholes on the bolt where the lock used to sit. Well, I guess I knew why no one had seen Danny's car, especially if he'd been in town for a while. What I didn't understand, was why no one had seen him lingering. With people like Dotty around, it seemed unbelievable someone would walk in unseen, let alone stay without raising any flags.

    I pulled one side of the double-door open, freezing for a moment as the familiar scent of beeswax and vanish washed over me. While Gramps handled all his projects in his shed, everything he had was stored here. There was nothing he loved more than wandering the car boot sales and second-hand stores, finding old furniture in need of restoration, and rescuing them, breathing new life into tired old pieces. He'd made something of a retirement hobby out of it, sometimes much to Gran's frustration.

    My breathing hitched as I saw all the furniture he had collected over the years. Old armoire wardrobes, battered units, and tables were piled high in a way that would have put even the most skilled tetras players to shame.

    I pulled the other door open, chuckling to see just enough room for a car. As Bastian pulled in, I ran my fingers over an antique desk with water-stained wood and a torn leather surface held in place by rusted studs, recalling the days of sanding, varnishing, and restoring, and remembering Gramps' kindly smile as I got underfoot and 'helped' in the way only a child could, by being completely and utterly in the way. A stick of beeswax found its way into my fingers until I was breathing in the scent. The urge to break out one of his unfinished projects consuming me.

I needed to feel close to them. I'd never got to say goodbye, never seen them since the day my parents forced me home and married me off to the man who had stalked me.

"You okay?" Bastian's strong arm wrapped around my shoulder, pulling me close. I wondered what he could see when he looked at me that made him feel the need to ask so frequently. I nodded pushing the door closed.

"I need to get a lock for that," I whispered, flinching as he leaned forward, slamming the bolt home.

"Now where's good for food? We'll grab something on the way, and I'll get some supplies as soon as you let me in on the lay of the land."

"You mean you don't have your phone?" I teased. Bastian was always on his phone with his siblings, but now I thought about it, I hadn't seen him use it once over the last three days.

"No. Thought I'd pick a new one up."

"Right, well, we can grab tea from Phoebe's, and I can show you where we'll be staying." I guided him towards the main road that led down the central route through the town, a strange sense of pride washing over me as he drew in a breath and whistled at his first real view of Barrett's Bay.

"I get it," he said. I turn to look at him curiously, watching his eyes drink in the majesty laid out before him. The gradual slope of the small town stretched before us, small houses dotting the winding streets. The ocean shimmered in the evening light, trapped within the horseshoe-shaped cove. I would never tire of seeing this sight.

It was the kind of view that left no question that magic existed.

Large cliffs surrounded the body of

water, where smaller rock formations and walkways created the perfect place for rock poolers to explore, and the dark, sandy beach would appease any holidaymaker, or it would have, if this little out of the way place ever found its way onto their radar. A few small boats bobbed idly in the cove, brought down from the beachfront boathouses with their bright, multi-coloured doors.

My gaze panned across the sand towards Grifters' Grove, a small collection of trees on the beach. Memories of Gramps' stories and great adventures always brought a smile to my face but now, as I looked upon it, I felt the weight in my stomach. I'd almost had my first kiss with Fate there, and eleven years later, it was in that very grove, he made his love for me known, taking me roughly against one of the trees.

My cheeks flamed at the memory. But as if summoned by my thoughts another vision froze me in my tracks. Grabbing Bastian's arm, I pulled him back to the building we'd just passed, using it as a barricade to shield us.

But even bricks couldn't stem my need to gaze upon him. I peered around the corner, watching, unable to tear my eyes away. I'd allow myself this one indulgence. Just this once, because I doubted I'd get the chance again.

Fate was handsome. No, handsome didn't come close. He was so damn gorgeous that it hurt to even look at him. Even though it had been less than a month since I last laid eyes on him, he still stole my breath. Each and every time I looked at him my mind and body went into overdrive, happy hormones flooded through me, as if just the sight of him could put the world to rights. But even as my body rejoiced, my heart burned.

The venom he'd spat didn't change the fact he was carved to perfection. The way his dark brown hair, with sun-kissed lowlights, fell forward into his ocean blue eyes made my fingers twitch with the memory of how it felt to push my hands through those luscious silky locks, how I'd grasp the back of his neck, trace my lips across his perfectly manicured scruff, and draw him down for the kind of kiss where nothing else existed.

Dark circles ringed his heavy-lashed eyes. He looked tired, and the small smile he offered to the lady he was speaking with didn't quite meet his eyes. It looked empty, hollow. The expression seemed alien on a face so normally filled with emotion. Part of me hoped he looked this way because he missed me, but people like Jesse Fateson didn't think twice about people like me, especially not when he thought I had betrayed him in the most hurtful way possible.

His broad shoulders sagged, dipped as if weighted by the woes of the world, an invisible burden bearing down on him, causing his posture to slouch.

I wanted nothing more than to sneak up behind him, inhale that fragrance of lavender and vanilla, slide my arms around his waist and hold him close to me. He made me feel alive, but now I also felt uneasy, restless whenever I thought of him. He'd given power to my deepest fears. I'd given him my heart, and he'd broken it.

My gaze raked over him, savouring his every contour, the way the outline of his muscles were visible through the fitted cut of his suit. The beautiful angles of his jaw emphasised by his dark scruff. There was nothing about the man before me that was flawed.

Jesse Fateson truly was perfection.

"That him?" Bastian asked, inclining his head towards the people just outside our view.

"Yeah, just ... let's wait a minute. I can't do this right now." I placed my hand to my stomach. "Maybe we can skip the pies and we can grab something later?" I pulled Bastian around the back of the building, taking the long way back down to my grandparents' cottage.

"Just curious, how are you planning on getting in?" Bastian asked as I swung open the small gate onto the gravel path. The scents of home, lavender and wildflowers, assailed my senses as I work my way towards the bay window, tucking my fingers under the windowsill. Biting back a scream as the sticky sinew of spider webs tangled between my fingers, I continued to probe until I found the small zip-tie bag Gramps had left there when I was young, in case I ever turned up and they weren't home.

I shook my hands, a squeal tearing from my lips, the bag flung to the ground as the eight-legged terror stared at me, its huge beady eyes sizing me up, ready to strike. With my arms flapping in some strange rendition of the chicken dance, I screamed and squealed trying to shake the spider away.

I heard the rumble of Bastian's laughter as he picked the bag up from the patch of lavender. "Is that some small-town tradition I don't know about? Was I meant to bring a goat to sacrifice or something?" The first genuine smile I'd seen since I returned spread across his lips as he joined me on the grass, making whooping noises, mimicking some tribal dance that would have had every cultural sensitivity committee screaming for censorship.

"Bastard," I teased, slapping his arm, using the contact as an excuse to ensure I'd wiped all the web away. He looked at me, his eyes shining with mirth. Taking a deep breath, I snatched the bag from his hand, making a show of wiping it down him first, just to be sure it was web free.

    He looked at me and smiled. I would have given almost anything to know the thought that had made his eyes light up like that.

## CHAPTER TEN

### Jesse

Three days. It had been three days since Jenny had called to say that they'd found her. Three days since I'd raced across the country on the four-hour drive to the hospital, only to find her gone. She was meant to be coming here, so what was taking so damn long? It was four hours away. Two-hundred-and-forty minutes. So why the hell was I walking the streets three days later with no sign of her?

The wait was driving me insane. Each minute that passed I became more certain that Jenny had been wrong. That the Sebastian guy wasn't the person she had she believed him to be. He was Avery's brother for fuck's sake, of course he was as corrupt and rotten as that no good lowlife. Jenny said they were half-brothers, but they had the same evil running through their veins.

A small commotion in $\pi r^2$ Away drew my attention. These last few days I'd walked the streets more times than I could count, circling constantly like a vulture. It only took a second for me to recognise the excited tones of Dotty's voice, but more interesting were the words coming out of her mouth.

"So I thought I'd take her some of your pies down. Gave us quite the scare up and vanishing like that, and I don't think I've ever seen Jesse look so distraught. Hopefully, the girl just needed a minute to clear her mind, can't say I blame her when she's used to people like her daddy." I heard Phoebe reply but not what she said. "Sure, I'll send her your way for a good old fashioned—oh, Detective." Dotty bustled through the door onto the cobbled pavement, her eyes bright with the smile she flashed my way. Her hand rose to pat her short, curled hair, the soft ivory tones of her purple rinse reflecting brightly in the fading light. "I hear Andy's back in town, glad you kids resolved whatever it was that's been eating you up."

She was back? When? How had I missed her coming home? I'd been parading these streets like a sentry, hoping to catch sight of her. "When did she get back?" My heart fluttered. I take back everything I thought about Sebastian. Maybe.

The way Dotty frowned made me think she'd thought I had already known. The cool October breeze whistled through the streets, carrying with it the cool mist that was rolling in from the ocean, making the pavement shimmer in the amber glow of the streetlight that flickered on behind us as the sun began its descent. I glanced at my watch, barely able to believe it was already half-six. "A few hours back."

"Let me take those." There was a

desperate edge to my voice, and if I heard it, I knew she had to. Her grip tightened on the boxes. "Dotty, I screwed up. I need an excuse to see her." She tsked at me. While no one but Doc and Rob knew exactly what went down between myself and Grace, or the situation surrounding how she left, enough people had seen her running through the street in tears after I threw her out of the surgery, to make their own assumptions.

I hated I had done that to her. More so now I knew she left for me, to keep me safe. After everything I had done, how badly I had hurt her, she'd still put my safety above her own, knowing what she would be going back to.

"Alright, but don't you go messing up that girl's head. She looked like death and that child's suffered enough. She deserves some peace, and you better not go ruining the only good place that girl's known." Damn it. How much did this woman know? It was like she had eyes and ears everywhere. "Last thing she needs is another man making her cry. I'm warning you, detective or no, you make her cry again and you'll answer to me. You're not too big, and I'm not too old to hand out a good old-fashioned ass-whooping."

She handed me the pies, chuntering another warning as she marched away, wrapping her hand-knitted cardigan around her homely figure. Being in Dotty's bad side was not a good place to be. Not at all. That woman had a glare that could level a city. I'd have to take a page out of my brother's books and drop by with some sweets to get back on her good graces.

But first, I glanced at the boxes in my hand. Two boxes. It seemed I was finally going to meet this Sebastian. Then I could decide if he was what he claimed to be. If I had even the slightest doubt, I'd shove him in our one-man cell so fast it would make his head spin.

The closer I got to the door, the quicker my heart began to thump. My hands were growing clammy, and I knew without a doubt it wasn't caused by the heat inside the boxes. I wondered if she'd had time to stock up on food yet. Maybe I should nip into the city, stock the fridge for her, make sure she had everything she could need. She was eating for two now after all.

But was she?

For the first time, I let myself think about the baby, and it was all I could do to swallow past the forming lump that constricted my throat. She'd spent a month with a bastard who'd hurt her for sport. She'd tried to take her own life. I pressed my forehead against the front door, closing my eyes.

Grace had proven herself to be strong. She'd survived Avery for eleven years, overcome addiction, escaped. She was damn near invincible, unbreakable. I had seen her struggle, and she won. She always won. Even if I hadn't known what she was fighting against. What had that bastard done to break her to the point that ending her life seemed to be the only way out? Or—a cold chill raced through me—what if it wasn't him to blame? What if my words had pushed her from the knife's edge she'd been precariously balancing on?

Fuck. I didn't deserve her forgiveness. But I was still going to beg for it. I was going to earn her trust, win her friendship, and hope I could one day be worthy of her love again.

I knocked on the door. I'd lost the right to let myself into her home the day I'd made her cry. Even if I had been sleeping there, now she was home things were different.

As the door swung in, I was greeted by a stranger. Black hair, dark eyes, his face turned from at ease to a scowl the moment he laid eyes on me. But my gaze didn't linger on him for long, it swept over his shoulder to where I'd seen movement.

A surge of anger shot through me as I saw the purple mark across her deathly pale complexion, and the telltale scab on her lip. She was hurt. That bastard had hurt her. The clover-green eyes that haunted my every moment locked with mine, and for a second I forgot how to breathe.

She was more beautiful than I remembered. How could my mind ever have hoped to capture a woman as radiant as her in all her fine detail? Her long brown hair clung to her ivory skin. She'd lost weight, she was too pale, but her cheeks were flushed the beautiful shade of pink they often were after a hot shower or when she—my gaze snapped back to the man in front of me. Who or what was he to Grace exactly?

He angled his shoulders, filling the doorway, blocking my view, but not before I'd seen the devastation morph her face, the first shimmer of tears on her cheek as she turned away from me.

My stomach dropped. She couldn't even bring herself to look at me.

"What?" The man before me straightened his chest puffing out. How I wanted to take him down a peg or two. No one spoke to me like that. His one word had been filled with disdain. He wasn't as tall or as broad as me. I could take him. I could drive him into the ground if need be, but more violence was the last thing Grace needed to be around.

"I'm here to see Andy."

"*Mira* has nothing to say to you."

"I think she can speak for herself." I angled myself to see over his shoulder, hating that the step up on the front door gave him a height advantage. "Andy," She didn't so much as glance in my direction, her gaze remained fixed on the blank television. "Grace, please." She glanced over her shoulder, tears running fresh tracks down her face. My heart squeezed painfully at the sight of her. I just needed her to let me hold her. Needed to feel her breath against my skin, the race of her pulse. I needed her in my arms, to give her comfort, beg forgiveness, but what right did I have? "I'm sorry. Please, just let me—"

"You should leave. If she wants to speak to you, I'm sure she knows where to find you. Or does the local detective plan on unlawful entry?" His eyes bore into me with malice. There was no way Grace was safe with him. He knew I was the law, and yet he seemed to be deliberately antagonising me. Or was he protecting her?

I exhaled sharply. He was right about one thing, though, I couldn't force this. I just damn well hated backing down, especially now she was almost within reach. "Dotty sent these." I lifted the box towards him, dropping my voice. "Is she doing okay?"

"I think you lost the right to ask that the minute you broke her heart."

His words struck me like a blow. His animosity made sense. He knew what had happened. "And who are you to speak for her?" Who was he that she would confide in him, share her pain?

"I'm the guy telling you to fuck off."

"Oh yeah, can you back up that threat?" I stepped forward, right up in the guy's face. I could take him, no problem. The back door slamming made me jump, my eyes snapping to the sofa. Empty.

Shit. I ran around the back of the house, hoping to catch up with her. I just needed five minutes. I just needed her to hear me out.

## Miranda

"That was pretty sneaky." Bastian chuckled

as he leaned against the open sliding doors between the kitchen and the sitting room, watching me with something akin to admiration. Okay, slamming the door, making him think I'd done a runner, had been childish, but I just couldn't bear to look at his chiselled perfection any longer, knowing that I'd never again feel the dusting of stubble around his jaw against my skin, or see his eyes looking at me with wonder and love.

"That pie?" Already with a fork in my hand, I gestured towards the box. The scent of Phoebe's steak and kidney pie made my stomach purr in delight. Maybe I could finally keep something down. Her pies were surely too delicious for my stomach to want to do anything but go into full lock-down. No way it would surrender this heavenly delight. It was almost seductive enough for me to be able to pretend Fate turning up at the door hadn't just shook me to the core.

"Yep, *my* pie." He flashed me his charming smile. It never failed to surprise me how easily Bastian flipped the switch on his personality. To everyone, he was this hard as nails, cold motherfucker, but the moment you became important to him, it was like something in him shifted from predator to protector. There was a kindness, a softness that only those he truly cared about saw.

"Do you really want to antagonise the pregna—" I sucked in a breath, placing my hand on the kitchen counter, my gaze dropping to the black and white tiles at my feet. Bastian was at my side in an instant, the pies forgotten, right until I ducked under his arm, and pivoted around him to snatch them from the counter, where he'd left it in his haste to reach me. Take that sucker.

God, I was feeling better already, and I'd only been home a few hours.

"You cheeky ..." He shook his head in amusement, following me into the sitting room. He lifted my legs over his, flicking the television on. I tucked into the pie. The normal explosion of flavours, instead of spurring my appetite, made my mouth turn dry. Still, I forced myself to swallow a whole mouthful before passing the box to him, seeing as he'd already devoured his. I swear Bastian inhaled food. One second it was there, the next it was gone. He glared into the box disapprovingly. "You're not eating." He speared a piece of the hot meat from the filling, holding it out to me. My stomach flipped. The saliva once absent from my mouth pooled, bringing with it an icy sweat. Springing to my feet, I ran to the downstairs bathroom, emptying my stomach. The cool touch of his hands against my neck as he held my hair made me sob. "Talk to me," he implored, rubbing my back with such tenderness the tears came too easily.

"I'm pregnant," I cried. I wasn't sure how I was going to explain this. I didn't even have the thoughts formed in my mind, just the pain, the raw pain that felt like barbed wire coiled around my chest, tightening. Any chance I had of making things right with Fate disappeared the moment I found out I was carrying John's child.

"I know, sweetheart." He pulled me

close to him, pressing my head against his chest until I could hear the thunderous sound of his heart. The repugnant stench of acidic vomit permeated the tiny room, and yet he didn't move. "We'll get through this, I'm here for you, whatever you need."

"It hurts ... it hurts so damn much." I cried. "I'm having John's baby. He'll never forgive me."

"Oh." His voice echoed with realisation. "Mira, if he loves you, none of that will matter." I felt his arms tighten around me. "And if not, then he's not worth your time. And your kid will be wonderful. It's got you for a mother, and you better believe I'm going to be the best damn uncle. You're not going to be alone, no matter what happens, I'll be by your side the whole way. I'll even change a nappy, not too many, mind you. Like one, and only if it's clean."

I choked out a laugh, clinging onto him tightly. He would make a damn good uncle; he'd been his Jake and Rosie's legal guardian since he turned nineteen. He'd done everything in his power to keep them safe, fed, and with a roof over their head. I was lucky to have him with me.

The problem was, I loved Fate more than life. His words had hurt me, but twenty days of being locked in four walls had given me a hell of a lot of time to think about what he'd said. Being trapped with only your thoughts driving you mad gave plenty of perspective. He'd been hurt, angry. I should have told him about John. In Fate's eyes, I had been guilty of everything he accused me of. Who could blame him for being furious? I remember how I reacted when I met Abigail. I had avoided him for a week. He had to chase me down to even get me to listen to him.

On the way here, I had made and scrapped a thousand plans. Had a thousand conversations playing in my mind. But they all ended the same way. We couldn't work. I'd still tell him the truth, tell him John and I were divorced, maybe salvage something of our friendship, even though it would hurt too much to ever be around him. But I couldn't ask for another chance. Because the moment I had seen him on the street I knew everything had changed.

I was pregnant with another man's child.

Just like his wife.

The ultimate betrayal.

Any chance we had died the moment John's seed took root in my womb. I dropped my hand to my stomach, to the little miracle growing within me. This baby would know nothing but love. I would give it the childhood I wished I'd had, the love I wanted. I would raise it like my grandparents would have raised me. But that didn't mean I didn't hurt. My heart was both elated and breaking. Because the man my soul cried for would never want me back.

## CHAPTER ELEVEN

### Miranda

I fell asleep on the sofa. Bastian had asked me to go to bed, but I needed this space. With the archway leading into the hall, and the sliding doors between the living room and kitchen open, I felt like I could breathe. Like I wasn't going to wake and, for one horrible moment, think I was back in that tiny room.

I still woke disoriented in the night, a moment of confusion consuming me as I searched each dark corner for the spider, but then I'd seen Bastian sleeping in the armchair. A silent sentry, watching over me even though I'd told him my grandparents' room was now his. He'd stirred at my movement, soothing me back to sleep.

I glanced towards the chair. Empty.

Closing my eyes, I listened to the quiet sounds of the cottage. He'd mentioned he was going to go out first thing and grab some crackers and light foods that I might have more luck keeping down. As if to reinforce my thoughts, the note he'd left on the coffee table caught my eye as I rose.

The world around me stretched and contorted like fairground mirrors as the sickly wave of nausea took over. I barely made it to the toilet before I was heaving. Seriously, little one, there was nothing in my stomach to expel. I cleaned my teeth, my stomach roiling at even the thought of food.

Air, that was what I needed. Some fresh sea air. It always made me feel better.

I glanced at the clock, quarter to eight.

Sliding my pumps on, I made my way outside, crossing the road down to the sands.

Sanctuary.

Serenity.

If ever there was peace to be found, it would be here, amongst the comforting sounds of the waves lapping the shore, caressing the rocks. It was like a soothing melody, a siren's song for the weary. I looked out across the quiet cove, watching the ripples of light on the ocean as I picked my way across the rock pools. The taste of sea air, the caress of the ocean wind, all carried with it a deep and soothing sense of peace.

It was strange to think that in times where the world seemed to be in chaos, there were still moments of tranquillity. Here I was, back in Barrett's Bay, while my ex-husband was God knows where, evading police on a countrywide manhunt. Even though the news had reported me as alive, no one but him would even think to look for me.

My world should have been crumbling. But if there was one thing I could do, it was survive. My fingers traced the dressing on my wrist. John had taken that will to live from me. But I was stronger now, I had to be. I wasn't just fighting for myself anymore. But the thoughts still plagued me. I had accepted death as my only escape, just as I had surrendered to my addiction that first day. John had a way of burying himself deep in my mind.

I was raw and hurting, and yet, while this turmoil churned within me, my gaze wandered to the rock pools, relishing the sight of the anemones and small crustaceans that awaited the rise of the waves to replenish the pools and guide them back to the water, and my mind travelled back to childhood; seeking comfort as it wandered to the days of brightly coloured buckets and raiding the rock pools, questioning how a rock tied to a piece of string could ever be bait for a crab.

Fate, Rob, and I would spend hours out here, exploring the rocks. I'd always been one of the boys, which was why I pretended the knighted spiders didn't scare the crap out of me, although I'd wager by the way I squealed and screamed whenever

## SAVING GRACE

I saw one, I hadn't fooled anyone. I remember how my hand shook as I sank my fingers beneath the water to fish out an enormous crab that had been blowing bubbles, which I thought meant it was in distress. These things were terrifying, with a temperament to rival any villain.

I swear, the boys made me do it just to hear me scream, but that didn't stop me chasing them across the shore with the mechanised monster before letting it return to the ocean. Honestly, I swear the first time I saw a crab, part of me half expected to peer into the shell to find a spider sitting in a small cockpit, chuckling maniacally while rubbing its mandibles together.

These were the kind of memories I wanted for my child. The pure, deep-rooted fear of armoured sea spiders, the secret treasure hunts, and tales of grifters and pirates. I had never known happiness until I came here, and I was determined, come what may, my child would know what it was to be loved.

I settled down on the rocks, my back

pressed against the cliff face where I knew the ocean spray would only caress during high tide. Closing my eyes, I let out a sigh.

When I had been in rehab, a lot of emphasis had been placed on meditation, but it was something I always struggled with, finding that quiet, calm place in a mind that was content to run a million miles an hour, a place that second-guessed every choice, conversation, or thought I'd ever had, while the little voice in the back of my mind told me I'd never amount to anything, that I would always be a failure, that the world would be a better place if I wasn't such a coward and—I cut off my thoughts taking a deep breath, my fingers once more caressing the dressing on my wrist.

I'd tried not think about it too much. It had been a desperate decision. Those four walls had been driving me insane, and it had been the only escape I could think of, the only choice still mine. It was a decision I wasn't going to dwell on because if there was one thing I knew for certain, it was that I wanted to live.

## SAVING GRACE

I inhaled and exhaled in time with the gentle crash of the waves, letting my head rest against the cliff so the early morning sun could warm my face.

The sound of movement, a rock scuffing beneath an almost masked footfall, made me startle. Eyes open, my hand shielding them from the sun, I scanned my surroundings until I saw the approaching figure.

Anger flashed through me.

It had been bad enough he'd called by last night, going head-to-head with Bastian in some strange pissing contest, but now he was here too. I suspected someone had let him know I'd returned, and he wanted to make sure there wasn't going to be any trouble, or maybe he'd wanted to warn me away again.

*But he brought pie.*

*No, Dotty bought pie, he just delivered it.*

So, what was he doing here? He had no reason to seek me out when he didn't want me. I wasn't hurting anything; I was just sitting here, taking in the sea air. Alone.

Minding my own business. The barbed wire around my chest tightened, stealing my breath.

*Please don't ask me to leave. I'm not strong enough to do this anywhere else.*

"Andy." Back to Andy now was it? Last night, I swear I heard him call me by the only name I ever wanted to hear on his lips. But I'd quickly convinced myself it had been nothing more than a trick of my foolish heart.

"What are you doing here?" This was his home, that's what. I was the impostor here. I'm the one who brought danger, but he didn't know about that. He didn't know anything. He still thought I just left. No wonder he wanted answers. I'd want to know why someone vanished for three weeks and then decided to come back with another man in tow, especially when he'd made it clear there was no place for me here anymore.

"I needed to know you're okay."

*Really?* I searched his expression, but the glare from the sun made it impossible to read. "Well, you've seen. So you can go."

I tried to keep the quiver from my voice. I needed him to leave. Needed him to stand by his words, his hatred because, in the long run, it would make this easier, it would hurt us both less. If I allowed him in, let him get close, the moment he found out about the baby it would destroy him. I couldn't watch him hurt, and I couldn't give myself the hope we could ever be something. It was too painful. Even being this close to him hurt.

He took two steps closer, his large frame towering over me, consuming the air around us. The man was walking temptation, and right now I needed him to walk away. Yet, I silently begged for him to stay.

No. He needed to leave.

If he stayed, I don't know if I could stop myself from tasting those lips one more time.

If he stayed, we'd have to talk.

If he stayed, I would find a way to make him love me, make this work.

And that wasn't fair. Even if he let me explain, if he saw past the anger, it still couldn't work. We would have a month or two at most, and we would both hurt more for it.

It didn't matter that as he edged closer his scent made my pulse race. We could never work. Not anymore.

"No," he growled, crouching so his eyes met mine.

Damn those ocean blue eyes. They were the things of dreams and fantasies. And that's precisely where they needed to stay, in a realm of fiction. "No?" I asked incredulously.

"I can see what you're doing. You're thinking about all the reasons we can't be together." A quiet gasp escaped me. These were not the words I was expecting to hear. What was he thinking? "I hurt you. I fucked up and I'll never be able to take that back. But couples fight. Your Gran and Gramps fought with the best of them, but they knew what they had was worth working on. Please, tell me you'll let me earn your forgiveness. Tell me you think we're worth the effort."

"Fate—" I blinked away tears. I hadn't

released how much my heart had longed to hear those words, how much I needed to know what we hadn't wasn't so worthless it could be easily cast aside. And yet, they were also the ones I feared most. As much as my heart rejoiced, its elation only caused it to fracture further. He couldn't ask this of me. We were doomed to fail.

"Stop telling yourself all the reasons we can't be together and listen to the reasons we can. I love you, Grace. You were the girl who left after the holidays but always lived in my heart, the one person I could never forget, the scale by which I measure everyone else against and found them wanting. I love you, Grace, and I can't bear the thought of not having you in my life. I know you feel this too." He grabbed my hand, pressing it against his chest. "My heart beats for you, my every breath whispers your name. If you'll let me try, I'll spend every day of the rest of my life proving to you how much I love you. Just, please, let me try."

His words brought tears to my eyes, made my lips tingle with the need to say yes. Instead, I pulled my hand from the firm muscles of his chest, dropping my gaze as silence consumed us. My tongue moistened my lips as I prepared the words in my mind. Tried to find the easiest way to make him see that what we had was already lost, that it could never be. Some ships weathered the storms, others were devastated by it. Our ship was already doomed, but as yet it hadn't accepted its fate. It was flailing on the water, hoping for a miracle that would never come.

Before I could speak, he pressed his lips to mine, silencing my objection. Almost as if he believed if I had no breath with which to protest, I wouldn't say the words he didn't wish to hear. I lifted my hands to push him away, but the traitorous appendages just splayed against his chest, relishing in the warmth of his firm muscles through his crisp white shirt. Any second now, I'd push him away. Any. Second.

His lips pressed firmer against mine, more determined as I tried to resist, tried to find the strength to break the connection.

# SAVING GRACE

I was weak.

My body melted against his as his tongue flicked the seam of my lips, teasing a near-silent whimper from me.

My protesting mind turned to mush, every coherent thought escaping as the scent and taste of him overpowered my every sense.

He groaned as I surrendered, kissing him back. Pulling him close, holding him tightly, as if to ensure he'd never pull away. I allowed myself to be swept away in everything his kiss offered. My fingers tangled in his hair, holding him against me, keeping him near. I'd allow myself this one kiss. A goodbye. Everyone deserved a goodbye. But with each second it continued, embers sparked to life, stirring a warmth within me, warning that this was not a goodbye, but a rebirth. Not the end, but a phoenix rising from the ashes. More brilliant and magnificent than ever before.

Passion and desire clouded my mind, derailed my thoughts of closure. This was the kind of kiss that consumed, not extinguished, and I was burning with need.

His hands traced over me in desperation, as if he needed to feel every last inch of me, reassure himself I was in his arms. When his fingers traced the waistline of my leggings I wanted to submit, to give myself to him, but—"I can't." I splayed my hands against that muscular chest of his, this time finding the strength to push against him while still chasing his mouth as he pulled away. I took a second to breathe. He couldn't kiss me like that. It wasn't fair. "I'm pregnant." The confession came out on a sigh.

"I know." He dropped a kiss on my head, pulling me against him, surrounding me with his strong arms and comforting scent. Home. This was what coming home felt like. What it felt to be loved, and safe, secure and wanted. His arms protected, and my heart hurt.

The warmth of his hand slipped down to rest on my stomach, his fingers caressing me softly in what seemed to be a silent promise.

I stiffened as his words and the meaning behind the touch registered. If he knew about the baby, knew about the betrayal, why did he hold me so tightly, as if he feared to let me slip from his grasp? "How?" How had he even found out?

"Rob told me the day you disappeared."

"The day I—" I pulled from his touch, rising to my feet too quickly, my body already trying to run. The day I disappeared? That wasn't possible. The world around me twisted. Danny had taken blood; he'd been giving me injections. Colours blurred, nausea burned and toiled within my stomach as I swayed. "That can't be ..." I backed away from him. My breathing shallow, the world making no sense. His arm slid around my waist as my knees buckled and I found myself being lifted into his arms.

"See, I still make you swoon," he teased. "Now, as much as I have faith in the hospital system, I want Rob to check you over."

"Fate."

"I'm sure we have a lot to talk about, but first, let me look after you the only way I know how. You've lost weight, and Bastian

says you're not eating," he continued talking, but my mind froze there.
 Bastian.
 He'd spoken to Bastian.

## CHAPTER TWELVE

### Miranda

My mind was all over the place. By the time I realised Fate had carried me all the way to the surgery, I was more confused than ever before. I thought back to John's mind games; the sherbet powder, the isolation, the spider, how he would wind me up until I couldn't take any more, until I would scream into the air, claw at the walls, scratch until I bled. He'd drive me until my nerves were on fire and then he'd hold me, soothe me, make me need his touch. But then he'd hurt me too.

Was the pregnancy another of his games? No. It couldn't be. If he'd thought for one moment I'd been with another man, that I was carrying a child that wasn't his, I don't know what he would have done. I sure as hell wouldn't have been allowed to keep it.

It had to be Danny. My blood tests must have told him about my condition and then he ... what? Decided he could turn it to his financial gain by pitching John with a fertility drug? If that wasn't what he'd been giving me, what the hell had he been injecting me with?

A swell of nausea crept over me, I managed to pull away enough from Fate to vomit on the ground in front of him.

"You know, if you have something against my shoes, you could just say." I saw the twinkle of amusement in his eyes and groaned, remembering our last reunion with him. I'd vomited over his shoes then too. I groaned, feeling the tremble start deep in my core.

A moment later he'd placed me in the

# SAVING GRACE

empty waiting room. Even my addled brain knew this wasn't right. I'd worked the surgery. There was always someone in here waiting to be seen. Fate grabbed a bottle of coke from behind the reception desk, passing it to me.

"Don't!" Rob's voice bordered on panic as I opened the bottle. The smell of soy sauce hit me as the bottle froze before my lips. "Caffeine's no good for the baby." His emerald green eyes held mine in a desperate plea not to expose him. Looked like he and Doc were still at it.

I rolled my eyes. Some things never change. Who was I to spoil his fun? He lifted the bottle from my hand, replacing the cap, returning a moment later with a specimen cup of water. Wrapping me in his arms, he pressed me against him firmly, breathing me in. "God, I missed you," he whispered. He pulled away, kissing my clammy head before offering me the container. I must have glared because he chuckled, pushing his hand through his sandy coloured hair. "We're out of paper cups." I'm pretty sure I didn't want to know what had happened to all the mugs.

Doc took that moment to make himself known. "It's all in hand," he assured. Oh, I knew what that meant. Doc liked nothing more than to trade surplus items with his other med school buddies. I swear, things went on under this roof that would make even the bravest auditor cry. I should know, I'd organised their accounts and inventory when I was last here. Doc's trading was the reason the storeroom was probably still overflowing with specimen cups.

I took a sip of the water, a warning look in my eyes. If this wasn't water, there would be hell to pay. The cold refreshing liquid caressed my tongue, sending a shiver of relief through me. Just water.

"You've lost weight," Rob observed. He crouched before me, his hands on my face as he gently turned my head, concern in his gaze as he studied me. Shit! I'd been so distracted by other things, I'd forgotten all about the bruises. I flinched, leaning away, suddenly very self-conscious as my tongue darted out to the slight cut on my lip. What was it about this place that made me forget myself?

Rob's cool fingers ran across my cheekbone. "Open." I opened my mouth without even thinking. Something about his doctor tone made it impossible to do anything but obey. He pulled something out of his bag. Next thing I knew, he was shining a light in my mouth, looking at my throat and cheeks. I felt like livestock. He placed a cuff around my arm, his gaze fixed on mine for a moment before dropping to the gauge as he placed his stethoscope on the crook of my elbow. "Hmm, your BP is a little low. Are you eating?"

I nod.

"She's hardly touching her food, and what little she has eaten over the last three days has come back up," Bastian's voice sounded from behind me. I turned to see him leaning against the surgery door and closed my eyes. How had he known I was here? "She's lost weight, unsteady on her feet too."

"Bastian!" I warned.

"She's also running warm," he added,

pushing from the door to make his way towards us.

"I'm not one of your cars," I grumbled as he moved to take a seat on the other side of me, taking my other hand in his. Great, now I was sandwiched between him and Fate, both of them holding my hand, making sure I couldn't sneak away. Although they seemed to be tolerating each other, I wondered what I had missed this morning.

"True. My cars never give me *this* much trouble."

"I could do with taking your measurements, then do you want to see the baby?"

My entire body stiffened. I didn't think that was possible at this stage. I glanced between Fate and Bastian. "How?"

"Well, last month Doc did some trading and got us one of those transvaginal ultrasound machines. The midwife loves it. We all got to attend a three-day training course. Well, me and Evie did. Doc went a little green at the thought."

"I did not. I just think there're some

things women feel better having done by other women. I'm a doctor not a gynaecologist." Doc grumbled from reception. I chuckled at his subtle Star Trek reference.

"You'll meet Evie another time, she's the area's midwife. You're going to need to drink some more for me. A full bladder will help the picture."

I eyed the cup, taking another sip, feeling the liquid slosh around in my empty stomach. "You think there's a problem?" I asked softly. I felt the way my muscles coiled at hearing me voice something I'd not even dared to think. Both Fate's and Bastian's grip on me tightened, almost as if they'd thought I was about to bolt. Was I? I realised I was staring behind me at the door, my muscles tense, ready for action. I released a breath, trying to force myself to relax.

"I think the hospital scheduled you one before you did a runner." His eyes dropped to my bandaged wrist. Oh my God, I'd been walking around here looking like a punching bag from Rocky with a bandage that screamed unstable. What the hell was wrong with me?

"Okay." My voice sounded small even to my ears.

He guided me through to his office. The large room hadn't changed at all in the last few weeks, not that I thought it would have. It looked pretty much like every doctor's office I'd ever seen, from the examination bed all the way to the desk positioned near the window.

"I want to ask how you've been, but you don't get abducted by your ex and come out smelling like roses." Damn it. I was beginning to think this town was the source all gossip came from. I could almost see the great rivers of hearsay congregating beneath the town, feeding its residence with all the titbits they could ever want. I assumed everyone thought I'd left, how the hell had—"Jesse went after you after his little display. When we couldn't find you, we discovered someone had been staying in your grandparents' attic. It wasn't a far leap to assume you left less than willingly. He never stopped looking for you. The minute

Jenny called to say you were in the hospital, he raced there like a bat out of hell, but you'd left. I don't think he's slept a wink the last three days waiting for you to show up."

I remembered how tired Fate looked when I saw him on the street. Had that really been because of me? Rob guided me to the scales, making a tsking noise at my weight. "How bad's the sickness?" I tensed as he moved to pull the door closed. As if seeing my reaction, he stopped and, without question, pushed the door back to its open position.

"Whoever called it morning sickness needs to be sued for faulty advertising." I gave him a tired smile. "Rob," my voice dropped to a whisper. I was scared to ask what I wanted to, to ask if I was really pregnant before being taken back to John. It shouldn't matter, but I needed to know. Tension rippled through me as my insides quaked. My nails dragged down the soft fabric of my cardigan.

"Oh, Andy." He gathered me into his arms and just held me. It seemed to be everyone's go-to response at the moment, and I sure as hell wasn't going to complain. Especially since I seemed to cry at the drop of a hat these days. It seemed like forever until he pulled away. "You don't know how much I needed that," he whispered.

I bit my lip, glancing towards the floor. "Rob, can you run my blood?" I asked softly.

"Sure, any reason?" he asked, jotting down some notes. From the look of the paper, it was the vitals he'd taken so far.

I exhaled slowly. "Danny made it seem like he was giving me fertility treatments. I didn't even know I was pregnant until—" my gaze dropped to my wrist. I flinched as I heard the loud crunch of Rob's pen as it snapped in half, his jaw set. "He spent the entire time I was there injecting me with something. I thought that's why I was feeling so sick. It didn't make me feel funny or anything but..."

I heard the small trolley being pulled towards me. "Keep drinking." I took another sip of water, turning my gaze towards the ceiling. "So, who's your bodyguard? NCA?"

"No, Bastian's John's half-brother." I saw the way his eyes snapped to mine. "He's one of the good ones. He looked out for me when he could. John's using his siblings as leverage."

"And now?" I winced as the needle pierced my skin. I turned my vision to the ceiling, just as I had every time he'd taken my blood in this room before. God, I hated needles. They made the itch beneath my skin worse and brought to the surface less than pleasant memories.

"I made sure they'll be safe." I wasn't ready to tell him why I thought this, but I'd get there. Eventually. Rob was easy to talk to, he was like the protective older brother I'd never had, and his light-hearted nature never failed to keep me smiling.

"Okay, we're done. Shall we take a look at little pomegranate?"

"Pomegranate?" I hopped up onto the examination bed as he patted it.

"You know the seeds, well that's about how big little Pom will be." I smiled as he touched my stomach lightly. Pom. That sure as hell beat calling it, It. Oh great, now my mind had capitalised that word all I could think about was terrifying clowns, storm drains, and eerie red balloons. I shook my head. Pom was perfect, it didn't have any eerie killer clown vibes attached to it whatsoever.

"Is it okay if Fate and Bastian see too?"

"Sure, I'll get set up, and once everything checks out, I'll give them a holler." He pulled a piece of equipment closer, pressing a button, initiating the loading screen. He unsealed something from a packet, fixing it in place. It was a good job he knew what he was doing because I hadn't got the faintest idea what anything did.

"And Doc if he wants. He got the equipment, it's only fair—" I froze. Hold on a minute. Had I really just invited a load of men to watch as Rob stuck a weird-looking E.T. finger up my—I cleared my throat, cheeks aflame.

"Okay, lie back."

Oh God, it really was going up there. I thought people used over the stomach ultrasounds. My embarrassment was forgotten the moment a grainy black and white image appeared on the monitor, and I had no idea what it was. Everything seemed fluid and blurry, like watching static on a TV screen. Giving up, I turned my focus to Rob, his emerald eyes were locked on the same nonsensical screen, a look of intense concentration warping his normally carefree features into something older, more serious.

Something was wrong.

Oh God, something was wrong.

I clenched my fists so tightly I felt the sting of the slice in my arm. They'd said it wasn't serious, that it looked worse than it was, but what if it had been, what if I'd hurt the baby I hadn't even known I was carrying?

My mind was racing, thoughts careening. I was pregnant before I had even left Barrett's Bay, pregnant when I thought the bag of sherbet had been drugs and had wanted to surrender to my addiction, pregnant every time I provoked John, every time I made him hurt me by not simply giving him what he wanted.

I blinked several times, my lungs burning with the need to breathe something more than the short sharp breaths I could manage.

I watched Rob with every bit of the intensity he gave the screen. The silence was stifling, punctuated by the occasional clicking sound as he pressed some button or other. The sudden chill of the room caused a shiver to expand from the very centre of my being.

With a slight sigh, heard as nothing more than a whisper, his eyes gravitated to mine. A smile broke out across his face that illuminated the room. A hundred-watt smile, bright and dazzling. My heart did all kinds of things I didn't understand at that second.

"There's our little Pom." There was such genuine happiness in his eyes that all my previous concerns vanished, swept away with the brilliance of his smile. "If you want, we can call people in now."

I didn't know how long I'd been holding my breath, probably since the moment he stuck that alien probe inside me, but when I released it, the need to pee burned in my bladder. I shouldn't have drunk so much water, but at least it had stayed down.

The small room filled too quickly, and I was suddenly all too aware of everything. My cheeks burned with embarrassment. Fate's hand engulfed mine, Bastian moved behind me, kissing my head, while Doc hung back near the open door. Rob went to great pains to show us the tiniest little dot on the screen. I hoped I wasn't the only one who couldn't see a thing.

Then something wondrous happened. With a smile, he flicked a switch as this rapid whooshing sound filled the air. No, not a whooshing sound. A heartbeat.

I felt Fate's grip tighten around mine and risked a glance. Ocean blue eyes shimmered with tears. I glanced to Bastian behind me as he squeezed my shoulders gently and I knew then, without a doubt, this baby would know more love than I had ever dreamt possible.

"From the measurements, you're around the six-week mark." He froze the image. An instant wave of relief washed over me again as he removed the probe, before showing me exactly where my little Pom was. I glanced to Fate, *our* little Pom. My chest constricted slightly. Ours.

Rob drew a circle with his finger over the image. Thank God, I wasn't the only one looking relieved at having the little blob pointed out to me. I barely dared to blink in case I lost the tiny little dot again.

I moved my free hand to Bastian's. "If you still want it, it looks like you've got a little competition for the title of best damn uncle," I whispered.

I saw a flash of emotion across his face before he glanced away. "Right, I should be off. I've got to check in on the terrible two." He cleared his throat, giving my shoulder a final squeeze before making his way towards the door, giving Doc the perfect opportunity to slip away before anyone could notice the slight misting of his eyes. The old softy. I saw him pull the hankie from his top pocket as he turned his back on us, thinking I didn't see him dab his eyes.

"I just need to grab a few things from the midwife's room, and we can finish up." That was Rob's way of saying, I'll let you and Fate have a moment. I smiled at him gratefully. His hand froze on the door handle, my gaze burning into it.

A relieved sigh parted my lips as his hand slid away, leaving it open. I wondered if a closed door was going to make my anxiety spike for the rest of my life, or if it would fade. John had done some pretty horrific things over the years to me. I liked to think they wouldn't haunt me outside of nightmares. This place, these people, made me feel strong. There was so much goodness here, it became hard to think about the bad.

Jesse Fateson was definitely one of the good. Just looking at the sexy scruff that peppered his perfect jaw was enough to set the world to rights. If I could bottle the feeling I got just from looking at him, I could forge a weapon for world peace. There'd be no wars, no strife, and probably no industry either given that I could literally sit and just stare at him, every minute of every day and always dread each blink, each fraction of a second where my heart pined for him. He was the kind of man you missed even when you were together, because you knew at one point, you'd be apart.

I had so much I needed to talk to him about. He seemed to know a lot already, and I wasn't not sure how he got the information, but he deserved to hear everything from me. But right now, there was only one thought. I placed my hand to my stomach, feeling his fingers intertwine with mine.

I had been sceptical when Fate said he knew about the baby, with Danny's injections and John's mind games, it wasn't that I thought he was lying, but I hadn't dared to have hope the father of my child would be the only man I would have chosen for myself. There was no doubt in my mind now the baby was Fate's, and whilst I couldn't express the relief I felt, it just added to the conversations we needed to have.

We hadn't used protection because I'd

told him I couldn't have children, and now he was going to be a father. I'd trapped him. Given him a child he'd not asked for, in a relationship that was still so new it should have training wheels. Yes, I loved him. He was my first love, the boy I had wanted to give my first kiss and my virginity to. I'd felt a spark between us, and it had only grown stronger when our paths crossed again back in August. But that was only two months ago.

I'd spent eleven years with John. He'd used and broken me. Why on Earth would a man like Jesse Fateson want something as damaged as me? Even when I let myself believe, closed my eyes, and just enjoyed being with him, I always had this lingering feeling it wouldn't last. That he'd realise how broken I was. People like Fate deserved perfection. Someone like me was only good as a placeholder until the perfect woman came along.

Now I was having his baby. It complicated things. He'd end up resenting me because he wouldn't want to walk away. What if the only reason he'd looked for me was because of his sense of morality? One of the things I loved about Fate was his integrity. Even as a teen, he always did what was right, no matter the cost to himself. I didn't want him to feel trapped, cheated out of a life he chose. If this wasn't what he wanted—

"Don't." Fate's lips fluttered softly against mine before he pressed my forehead to his, so the only thing I could see was the sincerity in those ocean blue eyes. "I hate I made you doubt us, that I see the way you're questioning everything." He cupped my face in his hands. "I'm sorry for what I said. I didn't mean a single goddamn word of it, Grace. You're not worthless, you're everything. Beyond value. You're one of the strongest, greatest people I know. I need you to give me another chance. I fucked up. I can't promise we'll never argue, but I can guarantee that I'll never stop fighting for you, for us.

"I'm sorry for what that bastard did to you. But this, you, me, the baby, how could you ever think something so wonderful could be something I'd regret? We'll take things slow. I'll earn your trust, make sure you never question that you, Grace, are not only everything I could ever want, but the only thing I'll ever want." He kissed me again, one of those supposedly chaste kisses that set my body ablaze and my heart soaring into orbit. "I only have one question." His eyebrows lowered, his face growing serious. "Can you please show me what I'm meant to be looking at on this thing? I've been a father for all of six weeks, and I've already lost our baby. That has to be some kind of record."

I laughed, a genuine laugh filled with relief and humour. Turning my attention back to the still image, my finger was poised, ready to—oh shit—my eyes traced the image looking for something, anything that could be our baby.

I tried to hide a sniffle. Stupid hormones. I couldn't even find our baby. I was looking right at it, somewhere there in a sea of black and white. A surge of relief flooded through me as I saw the little blip. "There," I whispered, not trusting my voice to disguise the emotions that had just stampeded through me. Fate grinned, his entire face brightening with the radiance of his smile.

God, he was gorgeous. I blushed, realising I'd just let out a girly sigh. I resisted the urge to pinch myself. If this was a dream, I had no intention of ever waking.

## CHAPTER THIRTEEN

### Miranda

After Rob had finished the check-up with some measurements of my stomach, he prescribed me some vitamins and some re-hydration drinks, and delivered me straight to Bastian who was waiting in the waiting room on one of the many comfortable seats. All still empty, I noticed. I had a sneaking suspicion my visit here had been planned.

Fate returned to work, while Bastian took me home to make the grossest, most unappetising drink I had ever had the displeasure of tasting. If I hadn't seen him make it from powder, I would have sworn he'd wrung the mucus from the bodies of a thousand slugs, and it didn't taste much better than it looked either.

I gagged on the first mouthful, shooting him an accusatory look. He was trying to kill me.

"Drink it all." He watched as I half-chewed, half-swallowed some more of the mixture. Placing the cup down at the side of the sofa, I fidgeted, pulling the cushion from behind me. No way was I drinking another lump of that slime. Not a chance in hell. No way. Forget it. "Did you sort things out with Jesse?"

"First-name terms now, is it?" I probed. I was curious what had happened between him forcibly denying him entry into my home last night, to their new, amicable relationship. He shrugged. Damn, looks like I wasn't getting any details from him then. "How are Jake and Rosie?"

"All good." He stood near the bay window, staring out at the incredible view. With my grandparent's cottage being directly opposite the beach, the view was nothing short of mesmerising, which is why Gramps had hand-built the two rocking chairs that had stood in the bay window for as long as I remembered. He and Gran always used to sit there in the evening, Gran would have one of her books out— the same books which had caused my innocent teenage cheeks to flush when I read them without her knowing—and Gramps would read the paper, do puzzles, or doodle plans for his next project. "This place is good for you, I get why you wanted to come here," he said with a nod.

"What do you mean?"

He shook his head softly, working his way back to the sofa, grabbing my glass from beneath the cushion to push it in my hand. Damn. I rolled my eyes.

"You're different here. You know, you act so well that it took you passing out in the bathroom for me to realise you were faking, but if I'd caught even a glimpse of you here, I'd have realised how fake it all was. Something about this place brings you to life. I'm seeing a side of you I never knew existed.

"When I found out what my brother was doing, I hated I'd not seen it. You'd played the role so well. But then I hated knowing because there wasn't a damn thing I could do about it. I've never felt more of a coward than when I realised what you were suffering but was powerless to intervene." He crouched before me, hands on my thighs, his brown eyes drinking me in. "I'm sorry, Mira. You deserved better."

"Bastian, we both did what we had to." We had both survived there the only way we knew how.

"Well, you know what you have to do now?" he asked seriously, his gaze still fixed on me. I shook my head. "Drink the damn drink." Yep, I actually groaned. I could think of a million other things that were more appetising than this slime, like casu marzu, the thought of eating cheese filled with fly poop, vomit, and maggots was *still* more appetising than this. Although I would probably feel differently if the choice was real. Maybe.

We spent the afternoon together on

the sofa, watching whatever movies were on TV, talking, chatting, and laughing. I'd always felt at ease with Bastian outside the view of the cameras, but there'd always been this tension. Fear, lingering on the peripheral of everything. I couldn't believe how different this felt.

He wrapped his arm around me, holding me close as we picked fun at the ancient special effects of awful movies that had since seen better days but were still riddled with charm.

As awful as that slime was, I felt a lot better for drinking it. Not that anyone would ever get me to admit such a thing aloud. The last thing I remember, before hearing a knock at the door, was some enormous animal laying rampage on a small country town.

I think it was more being gently eased off Bastian's shoulder, rather than the sound of the door that woke me, but the moment I heard Fate's voice my body snapped awake. I felt myself come alive, my fatigued focus becoming pinpoint acute. I swear, I could smell his unique scent from the door, carried on the salty sea air.

"You have got to be fucking kidding me," Bastian growled, throwing his hands up in the air. For a moment, as he grabbed the edge of the door, I thought he was about to slam it in Fate's face. "What the fuck do you want?"

"I made my intentions pretty damn clear last time we spoke."

"And I told you"—he jabbed his finger at Fate's chest—"I'd let you get her to the doctor's. Nothing else. You don't get a free pass here. She deserves better than you."

"You think I don't know that? But it's not your decision to make, and you do *not* want to be standing between us right now."

"Really, don't I? What you gonna do about it?" Bastian's hand ground into a fist, the muscles in his shoulders stiffening. Shit, this was escalating quickly. I thought they'd reached some kind of agreement before. I guess I was wrong.

"Bastian, it's okay. I want to see him, we've a lot to work out." My hand dropped to my stomach, caressing it lightly through my tank top. Yep, a lot to work out.

"Fine," he bit. "I wanted to check out the neighbouring towns anyway. But, Jesse, I'm only going to warn you once, you hurt her, I'll hurt your more, you follow?" Fate must have nodded or something because Bastian spoke again, his shoulders seeming to relax, but only slightly. "She's due another hydration drink, and don't let her try to convince you otherwise."

Bastard.

"I take back every nice thing I've ever said about you," I grumbled. A sudden thought invading my mind. "Hey, where are you going?"

He stepped back, turning toward me with a smile so brilliant it was as if he hadn't just been threatening the local police. "Phoebe promised me some pie and a tour of the must-see places. I'm hoping there's a gym somewhere here, otherwise ..." He patted his toned stomach meaningfully. His gaze tracked up and down Fate with disdain before he turned back to me. Watching him was like seeing Jekyll and Hyde, while he had only softness in his eyes when he looked at me, they grew callous and cold when dealing with Fate. "You kids have fun." He threw me a wink, although the moment Fate stepped into his line of sight his scowl returned.

Kids, please. He was the same age as me.

Bastian's shoulder bumped Fate's as they passed each other. "I meant what I said," he growled. "You fucking hurt her, it'll be the last thing you do."

The door closed, and Fate let out a chuckle, shaking his head. "I wasn't sure at first, but I like him. Now, what's this about you needing a drink?"

"Urg not you too. It's like eating Slimer's vomit and a slug cocktail, all blended into some torturous mess spewed from the very bowels of hell. If you care for me at all, have any mercy or kindness, you won't make me have one." Maybe watching those old movies had brought out the drama queen in me, but it was worth a shot.

"Aw, come on, it's not that bad." I watched as Fate vanished into the kitchen, rooting through the cupboards until he found the vile packets I thought I had done an admirable job of hiding in the bread bin. "Oh look, they do flavours."

The way he held his nose as he mixed it didn't convince me the flavoured vomit was going to be any better. If he thought I was going to put that stuff in my mouth willingly, he had another think coming. Seriously, he wasn't earning himself any points. He said we'd take things slow. Well, right now, looking at that slop, I was pretty certain I'd let it grind to a halt. What kind of person preached earning forgiveness, then made someone drink that? I crossed my arms with a huff.

Despite my attempt to ignore it, his deep rumbling chuckle had a direct line to my heart and did things to another part of me best left unmentioned when I was trying to make a stand.

"Come on now," he coaxed, taking my hand in his, gently stroking small circles with his thumb. Oh, that was low. How was I meant to say no when he looked at me like that? I swear, as he lifted those heavy eyelashes to move those smouldering, ocean blue eyes from my hand to my face, I heard the dying scream of my resistance, along with the snapping of pantie elastic on every woman in a thirty-mile radius.

"After you." I quirked my eyebrow as he extended the cup, the scent of artificial lemon already making me want to heave. He tipped the glass to his lips, his eyes remaining fixed on me. I gulped, watching the bob of his Adam's apple.

"Hmm, hey, that's not bad, actually. A little like cordial, texture's a bit odd but"— he shrugged, passing me the glass. Wrapping my fingers around it, I sniffed the contents dubiously, eyeing him for any signs of bluffing. He seemed genuine.

The semi-solid fluid oozed down my throat in what felt like a never-ending lump of pure evil, spurring the need to gag as the disgusting taste exploded on my tongue from the all too naïve and enthusiastic mouthful. "You bitch," I cursed between coughs as he laughed. Never play poker with Fate. Never.

"Yeah, tastes like the devil's semen licked straight from his sweaty ass."

# SAVING GRACE

Oh, that visual made me want to heave even more. "I don't even want to know how you know that."

"Tell you what," he disappeared into the kitchen, returning a moment later, "for every mouthful you have, I'll have one too. We'll suffer together."

Seemed fair. I suppose. It was his baby making me ill, after all. I tried to hide the smile that thought teased on my lips. "You knew it tasted like ass," I grumbled, taking a mouthful, watching as he did the same.

"*Everyone* knows it tastes like ass. There was a reason me and Rob used to call them devil's blowjobs when Mum wasn't listening."

"They make kids drink this stuff? Isn't that child cruelty?"

"It's the first thing you get when you get sickness and diarrhoea."

Yeah, okay. If you say so. When I got ill as a child, I got shut in my bedroom, made to sleep with the windows open—even in the middle of winter—and was left on my own to fight whatever bug I had, or die. Although I always thought my parents would have preferred the latter. I was lucky they didn't give me a bucket to use instead of the toilet.

The only reason I'd even had my appendix out was because the school nurse called the paramedics when I passed out playing netball. I'd been ill for days with the pain in my side and hot sweats. It was one of the few times I'd dared ask my parents for help, and their response had been to tell me to stop whining and get on with it. In the hospital, they had the nerve to imply their ten-year-old daughter hadn't said a thing about the pain she was in.

He grimaced as if privileged to my thoughts. How did everyone do that? "I sometimes forget what shitty parents you had."

"I don't know, neglect is looking like a blessing right about now," I teased. Shuddering as another glob went down.

"Hmm, the real blessing comes when you're good and take your medicine." The way his gaze dropped to my lips caused heat to coil in my stomach. His tongue traced his front teeth as he smiled. He drank the rest of his slime. I followed his lead. I'd follow this man anywhere, even into the worst torture my tongue had ever endured. I barely had a chance to finish the thought when he bent, lowering his lips to mine in a soft feather-light kiss. The sweet and nutty taste of his lips teased me with its seduction.

Kissing him was like a shot to my system. Electricity chased across my skin, causing a shudder to ripple through me. He swept his tongue over mine. I wanted to be annoyed that he'd had the foresight to have a mouthful of chocolate spread before drinking the foul water, but the contrast to the flavour I'd just devoured was too heavenly, especially when delivered by his kiss. I grasped either side of his collar, tugging him closer, preventing his attempt to pull back. I wasn't ready for this kiss to end. I needed this man more than my next breath.

He groaned as his tongue teased mine again. Sweet and soft became desperate and frantic in a heartbeat. I needed more, to be closer. Desire blazed within me, liquid heat pooling between my legs as my impatient fingers yanked at his collar, tearing the buttons from his shirt, sending them scattering across the plush carpet as I wrestled his shirt from him. The heat from his body set my own aflame. My fingertips traced the contours of his muscles before trailing down. He groaned, pressing himself into my touch as my hand dipped lower.

"Grace, you're making it hard to take things slow."

"I can see how hard I'm making it," I whispered teasingly, gently dragging my fingers across his erection through the fabric of his trousers. He pushed against my hand again, groaning softly, before I yanked his trousers and boxers down over his hips. I pushed against his torso, forcing him to step back enough for me to slide to my knees from the sofa, tracing my tongue across his velvety length.

His sharp intake of breath only encouraged me, while a glance up confirmed he was hesitant, unsure whether to push me away or surrender. I wasn't going to make this an easy decision. I sucked and licked along the veins and ridges, rediscovering every part of him, feasting hungrily. Teasing him until his breathing quickened. I took him in my mouth, swirling my tongue around his crown, moaning at the salty flavour of pre-cum, knowing the vibrations drove him wild.

He groaned, hands fisting my hair as I grasped the base of his erection, sliding my tight lips up and down his shaft in time with each pump of my hand, alternating between trapping him inside my mouth, and licking and sucking every inch of him. I drove him to the edge and back, until I felt his growing restlessness. I sucked hard, his groans encouraging me to work faster as I used my mouth and hands to drive him back to the edge. I grasped his ass, pulling him closer, thrusting his hard cock further into my mouth until tears prickled at the corners of my eyes.

His hands in my hair tightened as he tried to step back. "I'm gonna—" He tried to pull away again, my fingernails sank into his ass, squeezing, pinning him in place. My cheeks hollowed as I sucked him, using the flat on my tongue to massage his length. The vibrations of a deep hum in my throat was all he needed to send him over the edge. "Fuuuck, Grace," he growled. I looked up, watching him come apart as he exploded in my mouth, his ocean blue eyes momentarily turning blind from the power of his release. I lapped at him gently until, with a smile playing on my lips, he pulled his cock from my mouth.

"Better than a devil's blow job." I grinned, wiping the corner of my mouth, before making a quick show of sucking my finger. The reminder of what I'd done to him already making him begin to harden again.

He groaned, watching as I continued to lick my finger. "I wanted to come inside you," he pouted. Before I knew what was happening, he'd plucked me from the floor, his hands yanking down my leggings. "Turnabout's fair play," he warned. His hands sliding up from my ankles until he was spreading my legs. The wild, ravenous look in his eyes made it impossible to swallow.

He didn't waste time. He went straight for the kill, sucking hard on my clit. I cried out, arms stretched above my head, gripping the armrests as I lifted my hips, greedily seeking the pleasure only he could deliver. I needed this, needed him.

"You taste so damn good," he whispered, his hot breath sending tingles across my sensitive nerves. "Fuck, I missed this." He sucked again, stoking the flames into a full-on furnace.

"God, Fate!" I screamed. My body already trembling.

"I love it when you scream my name like that," he growled. My hips rolled against his mouth, his tongue torturing me slowly now. Forcing me to arch higher with each masterful lick. The man was sin incarnate, every dirty fantasy I'd ever had. I gasped as he pushed a finger inside me, using his other hand to hold me in place while he feasted. My mind was gone, lost in a flurry of sensations, licks, breath, thrusts. I writhed and begged. With him was the only place I ever wanted to be. Tears leaked from the corner of my eyes as his fingers and tongue worked in unison to drive me higher until I could take no more.

Energy crackled through me, snapping my spine straight as I screamed his name. Every muscle from my legs upward tensed as the orgasm crashed over me, flooding my vision with fireworks and lightning as he drew out the sensations before pulling away.

I heard the tearing of foil a second before he crawled up me. I could feel his hard cock pressed against my entrance. He was using a condom. He hadn't before, but he hadn't thought I could have children then either, and he'd known I was clean from my bloodwork. Now I was sullied. I tensed as the thought snaked its way into my mind. John's words, John's voice.

"Tell me to stop," he whispered, kissing away the tears that had leaked from my eyes. Closing my eyes, I shook my head. "Tell me to stop, or I'm going to bury myself inside you. I don't want you regretting it." He pressed his cock against my entrance in warning of what would happen if I remained silent. When my only response was biting my lip, he groaned, but still didn't move. "Tell me what you want."

"You," I whispered, not trusting the strength of my voice as those ocean blue eyes pinned me.

"Not good enough. Tell me what you want."

"You, inside me." I pushed against him, feeling his crown enter me. My legs wrapped around his waist, trying to pull him deeper.

"I'm going to fuck you so hard, so deep, you'll feel me there for days."

"Please," I begged. He didn't keep me waiting any longer. He thrust, sheathing himself inside me, burying himself balls deep with a growl that made my toes curl as my insides stretched to accommodate him as he filled me the way only he could.

"I've missed being inside you." He kissed my neck, sucking the sensitive flesh into his mouth. "I'm making you mine." He began to move, slowly, sliding out and driving himself home. My fingernails dug into the firm muscles of his back as his bare chest pressed against me. I wanted my top off, needed to feel his skin against mine. I struggled beneath him, tugging at the fabric until he helped tear it from me. "You're so beautiful, so perfect." I felt like he couldn't be close enough. My hips lifted, angling to drive him deeper, my hungry mouth lifting to capture his. He bit my lip gently, groaning as I rotated my hips, clenching my muscles to grasp his cock inside me harder. He was being so gentle. I knew what he was doing, we'd made love before, but slow and sweet was not what I needed right now.

"Harder," I moaned, thrusting my pelvis as he trailed kisses down my neck.

Harder, faster. I needed him to own me, dominate me, make me forget anyone else had ever been inside me. Each powerful thrust made my head spin, purged the memories of John from me until all I could see was ocean blue eyes.

The longer we were together, the more something changed in Fate. His eyes became determined, possessive as he powered into me. He wasn't just fucking me. Like he had said, he was making me his all over again. His eyes fixed on mine, flooded with lust, intensity, and love. He needed this as much as I did.

"Tell me who you belong to."

"You, Fate, I belong to you," I swore with complete sincerity.

He hammered into me, each brutal thrust sending tingles of bliss through me. It was more than before, more intense, more passionate, wilder, harder. His face was feverish, brimming with the same desperation and madness I felt, the desire to be owned and claimed, to give every inch of myself to him. We weren't making love, but we weren't fucking either. We were giving each other everything we were. It wasn't sex; it was a primal vow, a claiming, possession mingled with a promise of forever.

My insides burned, my muscles tightening again as I quivered and clenched, screaming his name as our orgasms collided with devastating force, leaving us both soaked in perspiration, panting. He collapsed on top of me for a second, crushing the breath from my lungs before he shifted, his quaking limbs somehow finding the strength to lift me until I was lying on top of him. My head resting against his shoulder.

"Fuck. I wanted to make love to you, not ravage you. You're really too much."

"You can ravage me any day," I answered breathlessly. Besides, we both knew there was more to what we'd just done than that.

"As much as I'd like to lie here with you longer, Bastian could be home any minute, and I don't want another man seeing you like this." His fingers caressed my burning cheeks. "Let's get you cleaned up." He traced his tongue up my neck. "Mmm, you always taste so good." Lifting me in his arms, he carried me upstairs, I froze as the bathroom door closed behind us. He must have felt me tense because the smile faded. "What is it? What's wrong?"

"Door," I whispered through the tightness in my chest. A look of realisation dawned on him. Without a word, he opened the door and at once my breathing calmed. I wondered how much Bastian had told him.

## CHAPTER FOURTEEN

### Miranda

I lay in Fate's arms in bed. Last night had been the first night I'd slept in the bedroom since returning home. I hadn't been able to face the confinement of the four walls, the feeling of their crushing presence. The room here was larger than the one I had been kept in, but I wasn't sure if my mind would even recognise it as my place of safety.

In Fate's embrace, though, my worries melted away. I only woke once, gasping for air. My gaze had snapped to the bedroom door, relieved to see it was open. Slipping from the bed, I had moved to the large bay window, taking the seat there to overlook the ocean and watched the way the dark waters shimmered in the pale moonlight. All that space, Fate sleeping, the smells of home, all soothed me.

I must have fallen asleep because when I felt myself being lifted into Fate's arms, dawn was breaking. He carried me back to bed. It was then I told him everything. I had sworn no more secrets, and I was going to make true on my word. Even if it had been a promise made only to myself.

I told him about John, how he had stalked me in school and the way that, when I was sixteen, my parents had held me while Mr Avery drugged me to ensure I wouldn't offer any resistance to the wedding. I spoke about how John got me hooked on drugs, about the first year being little more than a haze until they weaned me off enough to become a high-functioning addict, always crawling back to him for more.

I saw his anger as I told him as softly as

possible how drugs weren't the only way John controlled me, that he used mind games and fists to ensure I knew I was weak, that I was his property. I learnt to fake a smile, force laughs, be the perfect little princess his friends and workers wanted to see, while secretly knowing each underhanded deed they had done, or at least the ones they were paid for.

I kept the details light. He didn't need to know the extent of the abuse. But I told him about the withdrawal I suffered when John decided it was time for me to give him an heir, about how Jenny had approached me in rehab pretending to be just like me.

Then I spoke of the day Doctor Tavott found me here. How John had kept me trapped in the same four walls, teasing me with my addiction until I crumbled, only to find out it was another of his games. I told him how he'd reminded me how much I loved him, shown me how much he wanted me, and had Doctor Tavott visit me each day to inject me with something, playing us both so we would believe the baby was John's. I even told him about the spider, and why I'd thought suicide had been my only choice.

When my voice was hoarse, and I could talk no more, I braced myself. The little voice in the back of my mind goaded me, telling me he was about to walk. No one in the right mind would want to touch or be near someone with so much shit. My taint and stain would corrupt his perfection, he was better just wiping me off. I'd asked John to stay with me, more than once. I'd chosen his company, his touch, over the isolation. I deserved every ounce of my shame. Fate would be better walking away.

When I heard the covers rustle, I expected to see him rising from the bed, instead, he adjusted his position, pulling me onto him, holding me closer. His strong hands traced the curves of my back soothingly until my breathing calmed.

Daring a glance, I saw him watching me, chin tucked to his chest, eyes filled with pain and hurt. I lifted my chin. I wanted to kiss him, to know we were still okay, to feel if he still wanted me after everything he'd just heard. But I couldn't bring myself to. My mind was spinning, a million thoughts, a thousand troubles. Before I could look away, he captured my lips with his own, and we'd made love. Slow, sensual, healing. He used his body, his lips, his tongue, every part of him to show me how much he loved me, then held me as I drifted back off to sleep, comforting me with soft words.

I half expected him to not be there when I woke, that the time he lay awake, thinking about all I had told him, would make him realise I was disgusting, sullied, that he wanted no part of me.

Instead, the moment he sensed I was awake, he kissed my head before sliding out from under me to use the bathroom. I suspected he'd lay there, holding me until I woke, just to make sure I knew he wasn't going anywhere.

I slipped from the bedroom, already smelling the delicious aroma of bacon. Without waiting for Fate, I slipped on my housecoat and made my way downstairs, where Bastian was making himself at home in the kitchen. Dressed in his skinny fit black jeans and a plain black t-shirt, I just knew the moment he stepped outside the door heads were going to turn. Not only was he fresh meat, he was prime cut, with looks straight from a magazine and the kind of swagger that made heads turn.

"Morning, your drink's there." He inclined his head towards the work surface where the promised glass of devil's blowjob shuddered in the sunlight.

Urg. I'd hoped he'd forgotten.

I swear, I could actually see the rays of light streaming through the window bending around it in an attempt not to touch the stuff, and the colour was doing nothing to make me think of it by any name other than what the Fateson brothers had christened it.

"Gee, thanks." I don't think I could have sounded any less enthusiastic if I'd tried.

"Want bacon?"

"No, I'm good." But even as I said it, my eyes had fixed on the grill. He chuckled. Cracking an egg into the frying pan, moments later handing me a sandwich. "Thanks."

I pouted as he cut it in half, noticing the egg yolk was hard.

"No runny yolks now," he cautioned lightly.

I pursed my lips in a sulk. Was that even a thing? I guess I should get some books or something. "Hmm." I prodded the sandwich as Bastian grabbed some more bacon and started grilling it.

"There's an entire list of things you should try to avoid," he explained, looking ridiculously confident as he flipped the bacon. Was men cooking a thing these days? Last time I'd been here Fate and Rob had cooked for me, now Bastian. The world seemed different from when I was a teenager. Maybe men the world over had realised how sexy it was for a woman to watch them cook.

John never cooked. It had always been my job. Even though we had a housekeeper and chef, unless it was a special occasion, I was expected to feed him, although he binned what I made more times than he sat and ate what I provided. It wasn't like I was a bad cook, or I hadn't thought I was, the chef had even helped teach me. I guess my tastebuds just weren't as refined as John's.

"I've pinned it to the fridge." Bastian cleared his throat. Oops, I'd just been standing in the kitchen with the plate of food in my hand as my mind wandered. I glanced towards the fridge, and, sure enough, there was a printout telling me all the things I should avoid.

"Since when did you become an expert?"

"Honestly? Doctor Fateson gave it me." He placed a sandwich on a plate before making another. He slid it across the counter towards Fate. What was this, a peace offering? Oh, thank God, I didn't think I could take much more of the dick-measuring contest they seemed to have going on.

"Thanks." He grabbed the plate, moving to join me at the table, bringing the glass of devil's blowjob with him. I thought sliding it behind the bread bin would have

done the trick, but no. There was seriously going to be nothing getting past these two.
"I have to head to the city. I should be back around six." I got the distinct impression he was telling Bastian, not me.

"The city?"

"Ah, yeah. I was going to tell you, but ..." He took a mouthful of his sandwich. Delaying whatever news he hadn't delivered.

"Well?"

"I had to pull some favours so Jenny could have your body exhumed on the quiet without it crossing desks. I saw the file you left, I realised if the wrong people were made aware we were looking into you it could have been dangerous for you. I just happened to know someone who is close friends with the Commissioner of the Metropolitan Police. In return for their help, I had to make some ... compromises."

"What does that mean for you?"

"I've been reassigned."

"So, your workload has increased?" Great, there I was again, ruining his life.

The voice in my mind rejoiced with another evil victory, adding his job to the ever-growing list of things I was fucking up for him.

"Don't look at me like that. I came back here because I needed to get away, but I've never been a small-town cop, or at least, not a small town like this. I need to feel like I'm making a difference. The Major warned me this was an old man's posting, but I'm not going back to the precinct. I've been assigned to ROCU." His voice relayed an excitement reflected in his eyes and I took a breath.

It was a second later the acronym sank in. "Well, you certainly do that." I grinned, tapping that iconic boom, boom, clap tune before masking my smile with another bite of the sandwich.

Fate laughed. "I think you just found my theme song. Anyway, today is my orientation with our Regional Organised Crime Unit."

"Is that what you want?"

"You know, I think I can do some real good there."

My stomach sank as that little voice surfaced again, goading me. If Fate was leaving to pursue a new career it would only be a matter of time until he moved, where did that leave us? I wanted our child to know him, but I couldn't envision living anywhere but here, feeling safe anywhere but Barrett's Bay. Could we survive the distance? What if he grew bored with me, found someone else, needed something more than a two day a week girlfriend? He never asked for this, for me and my baggage. He'd said himself he hadn't been ready for children. What if he got to the city and found some put together, uncomplicated—

"Stop." His hand grasped mine, stilling the movement of fingernails against my arm. "Whatever you're worrying about, don't. Just talk to me."

"You're moving to the city?"

"No, it's a short commute. I have no intention of leaving this town when everything I want is right here." His lips brushed against my knuckles as he kept those ocean blue eyes fixed on me. "Now, if I don't want to be late for my first day, I better get a move on."

## CHAPTER FIFTEEN

Miranda

The next weeks passed in a flurry. Jenny opened a bank account for me, assuring the identity and name Andy Evans she had created when I first ran, had been designed to hold up to scrutiny. While she hadn't been able to offer witness protection, she had created an identity complete with past and national insurance number, which meant Doc was free to register my details accordingly when I returned to work for him at the surgery.

While Miranda Avery had been

brought back from the dead on national television, my face was everywhere since, as far as the law enforcement officers were concerned, I'd gone missing from the hospital.

It was a good job Barrett's Bay was a friendly community. People here looked out for their own. While there were things on the news that I would have been happier people not knowing about me, I knew not one of them would call the information hotline. The news painted me in a strange light, both a victim and villain with an expert hand.

While I hadn't seen Jenny, she was communicating with me through Fate. As the only person who knew I hadn't just run, or been abducted, from the hospital she was using someone called Weatherford as a go-between so as to have no direct contact. It all seemed very complicated, but as long as they were keeping my location secret, and the crooked cops who had seen me thought Bastian was being loyal to John, that was all that mattered. They wouldn't pay me any great attention because only John, and Mr Avery knew I was the one who handled the accounts. To everyone else, I was just the boss' wife, someone who smiled, deferred to him, and looked pretty on his arm.

I spent hours every day, between my wifely duties, ensuring that even the most anal-retentive, talented accountant wouldn't be able to see how I was directing their money to be cleaned. I was grateful John was too proud to let anyone think he had help. He had built his business from the ground up. Starting in school as a small-time dealer, then using his father's position at the bank to adjust certain customers' loans, allowing him to swoop in and buy the business as it entered administration. He then used these newly acquired businesses as fronts for cleaning money.

He had so many companies, shell companies, private businesses, that it made my head spin. By the time I was elbow deep in accounts, he was cleaning money for some very prolific people. He'd made a name for himself, and I got to balance the books for billions. With the headaches I had trying to ensure each contact had every penny accounted for, it was no wonder I was always chasing the high.

A cold shiver passed over me, and I once again thanked the universe for John's ego. If anyone were to have discovered I was the one ensuring their ill-gotten gains went undetected, there would be a price on my head now John had been exposed. Although whether it would be a kill order or forced recruitment, I didn't know. John had warned me countless times what would happen to me if someone found out what I was doing for him.

I wondered where John was now, if he had someone looking for me and Bastian, or if he'd stick to his plan and stay in hiding until the air cleared a little. Things were different than when that plan had been made. He thought I was carrying his baby now. A baby he'd been wanting for four years.

"You doing okay there?" Phoebe startled me from my thoughts before they could spiral any further. I dropped my hand from my arm where I'd once again been unconsciously scratching. Seemed everyone had picked up on my nervous habit now, and thanks to the news, they probably understood it too.

I breathed out a sigh. "Sorry, baby brain," I apologised, my hand now resting on my stomach. At eleven weeks, I now looked fat. Not pregnant. Fat. My once flat stomach had expanded just enough that I looked like I needed to lay off the pies. Speaking of which, I scooped another spoonful of the tart apple into my mouth, my eyes rolling back slightly in delight.

Phoebe made these mini delights just for me, her grandmother's recipe, apparently lower in sugar and unhealthy things, and exactly what little Pom was demanding. She was watching me with a grin as I perched on the stool near her counter, catching up on the events of the town.

I loved this little shop. The smell wafting from the kitchen at the back was heavenly, whereas the front had been laid out just like a dessert bar, complete with stool lined counter and a few metal tables near the large windows. Somehow it was both retro and modern at the same time.

The walls were decorated in pastel, flooded with hundreds of pictures of people, printed from the shop's social media page with people from all over the country posing with Phoebe's pie boxes. I swear, this little shop had more followers than some celebrities, and her online orders were phenomenal. She literally had to set a daily order limit, or risk being overwhelmed.

"So, maternity shopping, yes?" Her oak-brown eyes watched me expectantly. Damn, I bet she'd noticed my leggings *were* getting a little on the tight side. She'd been trying to get me to go shopping with her since I first turned up in town, but I hated the idea of leaving. The closest I got was going up to the garage where Bastian had parked his car. With Fate working away from the town, I was missing bumping into him like I used to.

I was fed up with rattling around the house after I got back from my few hours at the surgery and, as much as I loved

Bastian, I was finding the way that I was being passed from pillar to post somewhat annoying. There was never a moment where I was alone. I swear sometimes people even followed me into the goddamn bathroom. Okay, that had only happened twice, but it had still happened.

"Sure. Let me know when." Phoebe let out a squeal of delight, clapping her hands excitedly. "Right. I should head up to the garage, that table isn't going to fix itself." As I stood, Bastian, who'd at least shrunk back into the corner of the shop to give me some fleeting notion of privacy, rose to his feet.

For the last few weeks, I had been going to the garage and working on some of Gramps' old pieces. I needed something to keep me busy, or I was going to go insane. I wasn't sure of the cause, but my body felt wound tight. I couldn't read or watch TV. I had this constant need to keep my moving, because when I stopped, unless I was wrapped in Fate's arms, all I could feel was the encroaching anxiety.

I felt adrift, cast into turbulent waters reaching for a life preserve that was forever just out of reach. My mind kept circling to John. He still thought I was carrying his child. He was violent, possessive, and if he wasn't going to Bastian for updates, it meant he was getting them from somewhere else. He had to have eyes on me.

Paranoia was creeping in. I was scanning the faces of strangers, getting more on edge by the day. Every time I felt eyes upon me it sent an uneasy prickle chasing across my skin, even though I knew it was just the residents gossiping, behind raised hands, about the woman whose face still appeared on the evening news. Small towns like this rarely got a front seat to a nationwide news event.

I hated seeing my face on the screen, they'd chosen a photograph taken at a charity event I'd been forced to attend a couple of years back. I looked every part the meek and doting wife he liked me presented as. Every time the story of his manhunt and my disappearance appeared on the screen, I felt something inside me grow taut, tightening until I knew at one point it would break.

Part of me wondered if John was one of the reasons Fate had accepted the role in ROCU. While he couldn't work on John's case, there were many people he could look at, whose names he knew thanks to my binder, who John may reach out to or be seeking shelter with.

The only time my mind let go of these nagging worries, the paranoia, was when I was sanding. It was as if these physical burdens of labour pushed everything else aside for a moment. But I wasn't even allowed to varnish the damn things. The most Bastian would let me do was use sandpaper or the electric saw, and I could tell it was only a matter of time until he'd stop me doing that too. Besides, it wasn't as if I had the slightest clue of what I was doing. I'd helped Gramps, but only under instruction. So far all I had done was destroy a perfectly good table leg by taking too much off in an attempt to stop a wobble, and sanded a stain off a small dresser, leaving the wood with a noticeable dip.

Without Gramps, it just didn't feel the same. I didn't feel like I was achieving anything but a momentary distraction.

A growl of frustration rumbled in my throat as I threw my hands up in the air. What was the point in even going to the garage when all I would get for the next hour was an endless list of things I can't do? Don't lift this, don't twist like that. Ugh! I spun on my heel, marching back down the street towards the cove, trying to keep my frustrated scream silent as the flower Fate had left in the kitchen this morning was torn from my hair in a gust of wind.

A walk. That would help. I couldn't explain why I was feeling so damn antsy today. Even Bastian's goddamn breathing set my teeth on edge, to the point I was tempted to try smothering him just to keep him quiet. Every little thing was getting under my skin. Except Phoebe and pie. I rubbed the nape of my neck, my shoulders slumping as I was overcome with exhaustion.

Bastian's hands found my shoulders, massaging them gently as if he sensed what

## EMILY STORMBROOK

I needed. "You doing okay?" At his simple question, I broke down in tears.

    Stupid damn hormones.

## CHAPTER SIXTEEN

### Miranda

I was struggling. I knew the signs. My skin was burning, muscles were restless, and the itch just under my skin was growing stronger each day. I don't know what it was that had me so on edge. Things with Fate were amazing, and by some strange twist of fate, Bastian had reconnected with an old friend he hadn't seen for years, a girl no less.

For a few days he'd been stomping around like a bear with a sore head. Although he'd been promising to bring her by, and I thought maybe the distraction would do me good because, at the moment, I may not be trapped with the four walls of the white rooms, but I was feeling penned in.

If Bastian wasn't lingering, then Rob or Fate were never too far behind. I felt like some unwanted game of pass the parcel, or more like the bomb in those old cartoons being thrown from one person to another, and I was certainly ready to explode. I appreciated they were worried about me. But I felt smothered.

I looked at the flower on the kitchen counter and smiled. Fate was leaving before me each morning. He'd rise early, bring me a drink up to the bedroom along with some ginger biscuits, kiss my head, and tell me to have a nice day. It was the perfect start to any morning, unless we were both awake before his alarm sounded, and then there were other ways he'd leave me with a warm glow for the day.

For the last week, I'd heard him leave and moments later return to leave a flower on the kitchen counter. I wondered whose garden he was pinching them from and if he knew their meanings.

I tucked the heliotrope behind my ear, smiling knowing it meant eternal love. John always used to choose the flowers he gave me for a reason. It's why I knew some of their meanings. Just a few days ago he'd left me a blue salvia, its meaning, thinking of you. Although sweet, its appearance made my stomach churn, reminding me of the red ones John had left me in that awful room.

"Hey, is it okay if Liv stops by?" Bastian questioned, grabbing two bowls from the cupboard, and pouring some cereal. My sickness had pretty much gone now, I was back to eating like a normal human. A normal, fat human who was carrying pounds of extra weight around a stomach I had once worked so hard on keeping flat. Looking at it disgusted me and brought a burn of nausea to the back my throat, all spurred by how John had conditioned me to think about myself.

He had made sure I stuck to a strict exercise regime, not wanting any unsightly bulges, just smooth toned muscle. He weighed me weekly, and if I gained even a pound, the marker would come out, and he'd draw lines over all my imperfections, telling me to fix them, or he would. I thought I'd not let his words bother me, but every time I saw my stomach, I imagined a big black line around it. When I looked pregnant, got that beautifully shaped bump, I'd feel differently. I was sure of it.

Maybe a new face was exactly what I needed. Or some time alone. But it didn't seem like the latter was going to happen any time soon. I couldn't even go for a walk around the rock pools without someone in my shadow. "This is your home too, bring whoever you want here. If you need some privacy, you need only say." I winked.

Bastian placed a bowl before me, his ear already pressed to his phone. I swear I heard it ring outside. A moment later there was a knock at the door. There was a hushed, somewhat harsh sounding, exchange I couldn't quite hear before Bastian returned. I couldn't help but notice how at ease his hand seemed to be on the small of her back as he guided her through to the kitchen, even if his face did seem to hold the shadow of a frown.

"Sorry to interrupt your breakfast." The first thing I noticed about her was her posture. She stood like a soldier, feet hip-width apart, straight and confident. Her light brown hair had been secured in a messy bun, and she watched me closely, her gingerbread eyes taking in my every detail.

At once I felt like a blimpy, under-dressed mess, sitting in the kitchen in leggings that were too small for my growing belly and one of Fate's oversized t-shirts, whereas she was perfection. Perfectly put together in beautifully fitted black combats and a tank top that revealed a heart and flowers tattoo that coveredd her shoulder blade and shoulder. She looked like Lara Croft. She was just missing the layered ponytail she sported in the newer games, and a weapons holster. She sure as hell had the physique of the one-woman army.

"Andy." I offered the name everyone here but Fate called me, even Bastian had started using my alias instinctively. "It's nice to meet you. Have you eaten?" I gestured towards the table. Just because I was jealous of her perfectly trim, yet muscular physique didn't mean I was going to be a bitch about it. I knew how much work she would have put into looking like that, it's just, I glanced down at my stomach and sighed. The sooner it looked more like a baby bump and less like a pie belly, the better.

"Yes, ma'am." She nodded. "So, what is the plan?"

Plan?

"I need to run to town for supplies. I thought Andy could show you the sights." My eyes flicked from Liv to Bastian suspiciously. I knew Rob was helping at the clinic a few towns over this morning, Phoebe was picking her twin brother up from the airport, and Dotty was attending some meeting with the church. He hadn't seriously brought her here to babysit me while he ran errands, had he?

"You know, I am perfectly capable of being on my own." I tossed my spoon into the breakfast bowl, ignoring it as it hurtled from the white ceramic dish to clatter across the table, leaving a spray of milk in its wake. Palms pressed to the table, I rose, anger bristling barely below the surface. "I. Don't. Need. Babysitting," I ground out. This was ridiculous, I was a grown woman.

"That's not what—"

"Save it, Bastian. Since we arrived here, I've not been allowed a single minute to myself. I'm not going to cave if you look away for one minute. I'm not going to go running to the nearest dealer. I'm not going to meltdown or try to finish what I started." I flung my left arm up, showcasing the scar running up it. "Giving me space isn't going to send me over the edge.

"I couldn't breathe in that room. He was playing mind games all the fucking time, making me want him to stay, leaving a fucking tarantula loose every time he left me there alone." I heard the angry quiver in my voice and balled my hands into tight fists, fighting back the tears. "I couldn't sleep or eat. I couldn't even think straight. I was suffocating and drowning with no way out. All of you, I know you mean well, but you're smothering me." I'd never felt anger like that bubbling up inside me now.

"Andy—"

"Save it. I'm going for a walk." I slammed the back door behind me, focusing on my breathing, calming myself down. I'd barely reached the beach when I heard footsteps behind me. Surprisingly, it was Liv who fell into step beside me. Perfect step, matching my pace while staying a measured distance away, just beyond arm's length.

"I shouldn't have just turned up." She sighed. I eyed her dubiously, sinking to sit on the beach. She sat beside me, allowing me a moment of silence. Picking at the sand, I made it into tiny piles beside me before smoothing it out again until I trusted myself to speak.

"I'm sorry. I didn't mean to drag you into that. I'm sure Bastian's told you all about my past, it's why he wants you to keep an eye on me, right?"

"Actually, I really did just want a tour." She winced apologetically. "My father wants to open a training school near here. I wanted to scope out the terrain to take stock of the resources."

"Training school?"

"I'm an army brat. Father was a general, retired a few years back and opened a security training firm, of sorts. We have contracts from private security firms for our close protection courses, not to mention people who want to test their mettle with challenging team building exercises. We're only small, but we're renowned. Our firm is co-owned by Taylor Security Services, they're American-based, security to the stars and all that. My father served with its owner, and he helped with the seed money to get the business off the ground.

"I left the service last year to work with him. We're booked to capacity, so I've been scoping locations this way with the land we're looking for. We wanted to add some terrain challenges and from what I heard, this coast is amazing, I was hoping to find some climbing cliffs or coasteering runs I could incorporate. Bastian mentioned you grew up around here. It wasn't my intention to cause hostility."

I flushed with embarrassment. Shit, she really had just wanted a tour, and I'd acted like a dick. "No, I'm sorry." I huffed a sigh, placing my hand on my stomach. "I'd blame Pom here, but really, I'm just screwed up."

"We're all a little screwy sometimes. It's how we stay sane."

"So, Bastian hasn't told you anything?"

"Not a peep, but I've seen the news." Her honesty was refreshing. She wasn't skirting around what she knew, but she wasn't fishing for information either. Not that she needed to, I'd just outed my demons across the breakfast table.

"You still want that tour?" When she nodded, I got to my feet. "Sorry about the outburst." I apologised again. "Everyone's been a little over-protective since John is in the wind." I saw the way her eyes dropped to the scar on my arm, my hand instinctively moving to cover it. "He isn't a good man," I justified, keeping the story short.

As we walked, I told her the history of the area. It was nice to be doing something again, without some man thinking they had to play shadow. Every time I turned around, someone was there. It was a relief to be able to breathe, and Liv seemed nice.

I took her down some of the common hiking routes, pointing out the best vistas. This alone made me feel at ease. It took me back to my time with Gran and Gramps. They always had a story, although I am sure Gramps used to write fiction. There was no way in hell I was ever going to believe our cove was once a safe harbour for pirates. Still, it did kind of fit into his Grifters' Grove story.

By the time we reached the cliff walk, I was grinning. I'd had Liv chuckling along with Gramps' tales. I knew the moment she stopped, she understood why I had brought her here.

"Wow." She gasped, looking out over the sheer cliff faces. When she mentioned coasteering and climbing, I knew this place would catch her attention. Gramps had brought me here when I turned fifteen, said it used to be an old pirate proving ground where they learnt to climb with cutlasses clamped between their teeth. I knew his tales were as tall as Mount Everest, but I also recalled Rob telling me he and Fate used to jump the cliffs with the old youth club. Although if I remembered correctly, it closed well before I stopped coming here due to lack of funding.

"Is this what you're after?"

"This place is perfect. Is it privately owned?"

That I didn't know. Gramps often said the reason this place was never built up was that barons, lords, and pirate kings had brought up the acres, wanting to keep their homes remote. I told her as much before we started heading back.

I had more fun than I thought possible spending the day with Liv. It wasn't until we got home, only for Phoebe to turn up minutes later with pies, I realised I'd been played. Still, I'd had such a nice time, I wasn't about to ruin it. The long walk had done me the world of good, especially since I hadn't felt like I was being chaperoned.

Liv told me Bastian had texted her to say he was running late. I'm not sure where he kept disappearing to. Until now, I'd assumed he'd been sneaking off to meet her. Maybe he'd seen how badly I needed some time alone and, let's be honest, if he was leaving me with someone, he couldn't go wrong with a military-trained woman who now passed on skills in training people for personal security.

With Phoebe and Liv keeping me company, the three of us sat on the sofa and bonded over chick flicks, pies, fruit, and chocolate. I sat looking between the two of them. You wouldn't think they were strangers the way they teased each other. Part of me was hoping that Liv would stick around. I didn't recall ever seeing Bastian so at ease, so happy. Even if he was trying to hide it for some reason.

I felt some popcorn hit my face as a fit of giggles exploded. I grinned, realising I'd been daydreaming.

This was nice. Really nice.

## CHAPTER SEVENTEEN

### Miranda

The moment I saw the red salvia, the world closed in around me. I could only see that one thing, everything else was thrust into the background. I grabbed the kitchen counter, the vibrant red petals becoming blurred through the welling tears. I gasped, dragging a breath into my lungs.

*I'm not in that room.*
*I'm not in that room.*

But it didn't matter how many times I thought it, the barbed wire around my chest continued to tighten. My knees struck the tiles, the patter of tears on the floor becoming twisted into the scuttling of the spider's legs. I couldn't breathe. I couldn't move. Tears just streamed silently down my face as my vision grew darker. I wanted to shout for help, but it had never achieved anything before.

*I'm not in that room.*

My gaze fixed on the black and white tiles, I pressed my fingers to them, feeling their non-slip texture, forcing my mind to recognise they felt cool.

I flinched as the door closed, a strangled whisper the only sound I could make through my swollen throat.

"Sorry, left my keys." Fate's eyes snapped to me. "Hey, what's wrong?" He dropped to his knees, his arms wrapping around me as I went weak against him. My lungs expanded as his scent washed over me. He held me, rubbing my back gently until my breathing calmed and I felt ridiculous.

There I was, crying, all because he'd left me a flower. Fate didn't know what this flower represented, otherwise, he'd never have left it.

"Bad memories," I whispered, gesturing towards the kitchen surface. He straightened to look at the counter, still holding me close.

"Motherfucker," he snarled.

"What's going on?" Bastian questioned, sauntering into the kitchen in just his pyjama bottoms, rubbing a hand through his wet hair.

"He's been in the fucking house." Fate raged, he gestured towards the flower. "He was fucking here."

I stiffened. A cold sweat breaking out over my skin. "They've not been from you?"

"There's been more than one?" he growled. He pulled his phone from his pocket, holding a finger up towards me. "Capitan, it's me. I'm not coming in. I'll fill you in later."

Taking my arm, he helped me to stand, guiding me to sit at the table, flicking the kettle on.

"What's going on?" My heart beat

against my ribs with sickening force. Fate looked enraged; his concern shielded by the anger in his eyes but so clear in his actions. The way he kept touching me, rubbing my back, stroking my hair, holding my hand, all warned me of the danger.

Bastian clicked the grill on, slipping some toast beneath it. "Eat first."

"He's here, isn't he?" I heard the quiver in my voice. "Oh, God. He's here." I covered my mouth my hands trembling. Suddenly everything was making more sense, the twenty-four seven guard, Bastian's disappearances. "You've been meeting with him? How long?" I rose to my feet, betrayal nestling in my chest. "How long have you known?"

"A couple of weeks." Fate placed his hands on my arms, keeping those calming ocean blue eyes on mine.

Except they weren't calming. They were filled with fury and remorse. "A couple of weeks!" I echo in rage. All the times I'd thought I'd felt eyes on me, the uneasy feeling gnawing in my gut. My body had been trying to warn me he was here.

"What the actual fuck?" I pushed Fate away from me, barely making it to the sink before I vomited. John was here. Oh God. My trembling hands fought to unscrew the lid of the mouthwash.

"We didn't want you worrying about this."

"Worrying? Really, that's what you're going with? The man who kept me locked in a box room for three weeks while fucking with my head turns up, and you don't think I need to know?" My accusatory gaze snaps to Bastian. "And you! You've been meeting with him? You better start talking. Right. Now." I didn't miss the way his gaze deferred to Fate.

"Okay, but you have to promise to stay calm. Stress is bad for the baby."

Calm? Were they fucking kidding me right now? They wanted me to stay calm?

"We don't know where he's hiding out, but it's not in town. Dotty saw someone meeting his description a fortnight back. He left a note with the post asking me to meet. I was hoping he'd just move on and go back into hiding."

Concern knotted my stomach. If he'd been watching us, he knew about me and Fate. Was this why I'd hardly seen him the last few weeks, had he been keeping his distance?

"It's okay," Bastian soothed as if reading my mind. "He thinks we're renting a room here from Jesse so we can keep an eye on the local police." I paced the kitchen, pushing my hands through my hair. This wasn't good. My skin was on fire, my feet burning with the need to run. I brought him here. I hadn't thought for one moment he'd come. It went against the plan. We should have been safe here.

"What does he want?"

"You know the answer to that," Bastian answered honestly. He was right, I did. John had always had an unhealthy obsession with me. But if he was here, why hadn't he just come and taken me into hiding with him? That would be his end goal. So why the flowers, the waiting around? It didn't make sense.

"Look, until we've pinned him down, I don't want you going anywhere alone, okay?" Fate asked, pulling me into his arms, stilling my nervous movements. I nodded against his chest. "We're close to finding him. Just, try to relax, let us handle this." Fate inclined his head to Bastian who, taking the hint, left.

As the front door closed, Fate lifted me onto the kitchen counter, much like Gran used to whenever I'd hurt myself.

"It's going to be okay," he comforted, pressing his forehead against mine. "I need you to take some deep breaths for me, okay." I could feel the way I was trembling, but no matter how many breaths I took, I couldn't shed the tension, couldn't still the chattering of my teeth, or the tightness that spread painfully across my chest. I couldn't go back. I just couldn't. His hand stilled my fingers as they scratched my arm.

He leaned forward and kissed me, but there was nothing gentle about this kiss. It was raw, just like me, flooding my veins with energy. Fate always kissed like he owned me. There was never anything shy or reserved. He possessed, dominated, and stole every breath from my lungs, and

I gave him everything willingly.

His tongue stroked mine, his fingers curled around the nape of my neck in a gesture both possessive and protective as he claimed my mouth. "I know a way to ease that tension." His voice became deep, like sex and sin against my lips. Grasping my hips, he pulled me to the edge of the counter, snatching my leggings down. He kissed me again, a possessive need in each and every stroke of his tongue against mine.

My arms circled his neck, drawing him against me, my lungs inflating with need and desire. Fate's breath hitched as he drove his finger inside me, hard and fast, his lips remaining against mine, capturing and swallowing every moan he stirred. He moved with precision, stretching and teasing every sensitive nerve, hitting each spot of pleasure like a master, driving me closer to release.

I rocked against him; I was so close. So close. I needed more, more pressure, more contact, more Fate. Sensing my urgency, his fingers stilled, sliding from inside me. His deep rumbling chuckle vibrated as I cursed him.

Dropping to his knees, he slid my legs over his shoulders. His scruff sent a burn of pleasure up the inside of my thigh as he buried his face between my legs. I ached with need; it coiled inside me tightly, like a serpent ready to strike. My muscles grew rigid, taut, lungs burned with the need to breathe, but his assault on me was relentless, keeping me gasping, short sharp intakes of breath between a frenzy of pleasure. My hips bucked, pressing myself harder into his skilled mouth.

His slick finger returned, impaling me, filling the empty void that was crying for him, flooding my vision with shooting stars. He possessed me completely, overwhelming my every sense, his fingers thrusting, his tongue lapping sending starbursts and fireworks through my soul.

My elbows barely seemed to support my weight, my head fell back, body quivering as he feasted on me. "Fate." I barely forced his name through trembling lips as I came apart around him, my muscles gripping him as he continued to stroke and thrust, riding my orgasm with his fingers until he'd taken everything from me.

"Feel better?" he asked, a mischievous twinkle brightening the ocean blue eyes filled with lust and worry.

My eyes dropped to the bulge straining against his trousers. I grasped his tie, pulling him back towards me, reclaiming his mouth, tasting myself on his tongue.

I was feeling a little better, but I was nowhere near done with him yet.

## CHAPTER EIGHTEEN

Miranda

The next few days were tense. Fate was back at work, using his resources to determine possible places John could be hiding. I hated the thought of him being so close. But now I got up with Fate, the flowers had stopped appearing on the kitchen counter. The thought John had let himself into my home left me on edge, my skin crawling. I hadn't slept well for days, which was why this morning, I'd had a hard time waking up and around lunchtime had crawled back into bed for a nap.

It was a soft bang that partially roused me from my sleep, that, and the feeling of the quilt moving as Fate slid into the bottom of the bed, his hot mouth seeking my body trailing soft kisses up my thighs. Grabbing the pillow, I pressed it over my face, stifling my moans so Bastian wouldn't hear as Fate's tongue lashed at my clit greedily. My body arched into him, hungry for his touch. Pregnancy seemed to have heightened every sense, making even the slightest sensation more intense.

My stomach tightened as his smooth chin brushed against the inside of my thigh.

Smooth chin.

I froze, a scream tearing from my lips. I scooted up the bed, legs flailing as two firm hands grasped my ankles, yanking me back down as I wailed.

"Missed you, baby."

Fuck. No. This couldn't be happening.

"Bastian!" I shrieked, trying to kick John off me. His hands grasped my ankles harder, sending a splinter of pain shooting up my legs. "No!" I screamed, the bed creaking as I twisted and bucked.

"I can't believe you let another man touch you." His fingers thrust roughly inside me. "This belongs to me." I heard him grunt as my knee connected with his temple, enough to loosen his grip. I yanked from his grasp, scrambling off the bed, running for the open door. Burning pain exploded across my scalp as his hand wrapped around my hair, snatching me back to him. Air whooshed from my lungs as my collarbone struck the bedpost so hard I struggled to breathe. I staggered back towards the door, but he caught me around the waist, flinging me back onto the bed with such force I bounced.

"Bastian!" I cried again through gasping sobs.

"Oh, he's not coming. My own brother knew you were fucking the cop and stayed quiet. How do you think that makes me feel, Miranda?" His hand collared my throat. "How do you think it felt, watching him fuck you on the kitchen counter, hearing you scream his name like a two-bit whore? How long has it been going on, hmm?" His fingers squeezed around my throat. My nails sunk into his flesh as I fought to claw myself free, but he only pressed harder.

"Let me go," I rasped.

"You clearly don't understand the fucking situation, Miranda. You let another man touch you. Another man trespass on what's mine. You're no longer pure. You're tainted, dirtied by another man. Do you think it can go unpunished?"

The edges of my vision darkened. Each strike becoming weaker as I failed to fend him off.

No. This can't be the end.

I can't die like this.

What about the baby?

What about Fate?

I kept hitting, knowing the moment I stopped struggling it was over. I always knew one day he was going to kill me. It had been ingrained in my mind for years. But I thought I'd finally escaped. I kicked and clawed, scratched and bucked. But he was bigger and stronger than me in every way.

I could hear the pathetic rasping sound as I tried to breathe, as I dragged air through my restricted airways and attempted to beg for my life. But his eyes. I've never seen eyes like that before. He was crazed, maddened. Possession and fury burnt like hellfire, kindling destruction and hatred.

"Was he good?" he growled, shaking me like a rag doll. He pressed his knees between my thighs. "I had you first, I'll have you last as well." I heard his zipper. Tears streamed from my eyes and I prayed it would be over soon. "You were mine. Why did you do this to us? You sullied yourself, you sullied our baby. Why?" he demanded, as if he thought I could answer through his crushing grip. "Why did—" an explosion echoed around my ears. I watched in a daze as John jerked, falling sideways. Yet it still felt as though his hands were wrapped around my throat. I could still feel the pressure of his nails even as vomit bubbled up.

My breathing rattled again, wheezing as I choked weakly on the vomit, all too aware of the wetness spreading down my thighs as my bladder emptied.

"You're okay, Andy."

I screamed as someone touched me, or at least I tried to, but no sound escaped me. I lashed out, my gaze too unfocused to make out anything but a shape, my heart thundering too loud to recognise the voice through the madness. "I've called Rob. Hey, you're okay." I felt hands run through my hair and realised I was no longer flailing, that my body was heavy, unresponsive. Was it dark, night time maybe? My thoughts drifted as heaviness pressed down on me. "Stay awake, Andy. Breathe slowly." Gingerbread coloured eyes held my fading gaze. I couldn't remember who they belonged to, but they made me feel calm. Like I could sleep.

"Where is she?" I heard Rob's voice at the door. "Ambulance is en route. Doc's with Bastian. Andy, can you hear me?" I tried to force my eyelids open, but for the effort it took I may as well have been trying to lift weights well beyond my ability. Rob's distorted form stood over me, white as a sheet. For a second, as I managed the tiniest of breaths through my nose, I could smell the combined odour of vomit and urine. "Keep your eyes on me." I felt his fingers examining my throat. God, it hurt to breathe. I held my breath for a second, hoping to find relief, panicking as I couldn't inhale again. The world twisted on its axis. "I'm going to intubate." The words drifted around my mind as I sank into darkness.

## Jesse

"Fuck!" I drove my fist into the brick wall by the vending machine. Again and again, until blood soaked my knuckles and I'd screamed myself hoarse with strings of profanities I hadn't even known I was capable of. I'd seen a flurry of movement, people scurrying away to put as much distance between them and the crazy new guy as possible. "Goddammit!" I screamed, kicking the vending machine, sending a precariously balanced chocolate bar plummeting to freedom.

Rage bubbled inside me, consuming

me like a living, breathing force. Tainting my vision with its fury. I needed something to hit, something to hurt, because, Goddammit, I'd failed to protect the one person I should have been watching over.

Someone was brave. Through the roaring in my head, I heard a marching footfall, a murmur of conversation unheard as my fist found the wall once more. Pain burned through my split and bloody knuckles. But it wasn't helping. The pressure in my chest wasn't easing. I'd fucking failed her. Came to work knowing he was out there, knowing he was close. "Fuuuck!"

Behind me, Martin, picked up my broken phone, from where I'd flung it against the wall after Rob had called.

My boss. I was losing it in front of my boss, and all I could think about was how he better be well-trained. I was holding onto my control by a thread, and anywhere near me was not the best place to be right now.

"Wanna talk about it?"

Martin was the head of the ROCU

division. He was the kind of manager that turned a team into a family, rather than pitting them against each other to win favour. I'd only known him a few weeks, and the man had already earned my respect. I owed him more than laying siege to our headquarters, but fuck. I screwed up. I thought she'd be safe. Just as I was about to swing again, he grabbed my wrist, placing himself between me and the wall. He was either damned brave or a fucking fool. His eyes locked with mine, his posture adapted. He took control of me like he was a handler, and I the rabid dog under his charge.

I dropped my gaze. "Grace is in hospital."

"The baby?" he asked, fishing into his jacket pocket for his keys, before gesturing towards the front of the building. He lifted his hand, gesturing away the security officers who must have been waiting for me to tire myself out before making a move. They'd have been waiting a long damn time. I was nothing but a ball of rage and energy, each emotion feeding and sustaining the other.

"She's on a machine to keep her breathing." I push my hands through my hair, kicking out at the machine again, a frustrated roar tearing from my throat. I couldn't lose her. I needed her. She couldn't leave me.

*Please don't leave me.*

"Then what are we doing here? Come on, I'll give you a ride." Martin dialled a number on his phone, saying something I didn't catch. "Do you know what happened?" His hand fell on my shoulder, steering me away from the blood-streaked wall.

"Her bastard ex."

"Jealous?"

"Abusive. John Fucking Avery." Even his name felt like acid on my tongue. That fucking bastard had been in our home. Again. And the idiot I was had left her there. I thought Bastian would have been enough to keep her safe. I'd been a fucking idiot. Bad guys didn't play by the rules. They wrote their own playbook. I shouldn't have expected anything less. I should have known something like this would happen.

I should have been there.

I saw Martin stiffen beside me. Everyone knew Avery's name now. He was infamous. "I thought his wife was off the grid, disappeared from the hospi—oh bloody hell, you've been hiding her? Your Grace is Miranda Avery?" He bit off a curse, clearly holding back more questions. He knew there would be no simple answers.

"She went into hiding. She's an informant. It had to look like she was staying loyal, following his protocol. He should have stayed away. She should have been safe."

"Did they at least get the fucker?"

"Fuck! I don't know." My leg lashed out connecting with a bin sending it toppling. My ears pretty much stopped working when I heard the sirens and Rob saying Avery had been in the house and he was going with Grace to the hospital. That she wasn't breathing on her own. "I should have been there." I cursed again. "I knew he was lurking."

My hands balled into fists. Jenny had told me there was a plan. That she'd gathered a few faces she knew she could trust. That the next time Avery poked his head from whatever hole he'd been hiding in they were going to bury him. What the fuck had happened to those promises? We'd been talking for weeks. She assured me Grace would be safe.

But she wasn't, was she? She was on her way to hospital with a machine fucking breathing for her. That wasn't safe.

Fuck.

"Look. I'm gonna need you to calm down. This car's a rental. Do you have any idea how hard it is to find a decent garage around here?" He pressed the clicker for the car. Martin was a tall man, six foot five at least, and built like a brick wall, so watching him cram his frame into the small two-door courtesy car should have lifted my mood a little. But it didn't.

The only thing racing through my mind was the call from Rob. I don't think I'd ever heard him sound so worried. He was riding in the ambulance. He'd had to intubate her when she'd stopped breathing.

She'd stopped fucking breathing.

My thoughts kept returning to this one sentence. It played on loop, haunting me. I blinked back the mist in my eyes. That fucker almost killed her.

*Please let it be almost.*

I didn't know whether I wanted him to be dead, or if I needed to crush the life from him myself. One thing was certain, if he'd survived, he sure as hell wouldn't live to see the inside of a jail. Not when I got my hands on him.

"Hey, she'll be okay. Your brother's with her right?"

"Avery came into her home."

"How?"

I took a breath, trying to calm myself down, and failing. "She has this thing about locked doors. He kept her prisoner for eleven years. She won't lock the doors. The fucker strolled right in, shot his brother, and tried to kill my ... I should have been there." The rage was leaving, failure and dejection filling the void it left. It was my job to keep her safe.

"If you'd been there, he'd likely have shot you too. How's the brother?"

Fuck. I hadn't even asked. All I could think about was Grace. She'd stopped breathing.

I don't remember the rest of the car ride. At some point, I'd yanked my tie off, loosened my top buttons, it was so damn hard to breathe. All I kept seeing was that bastard's hands wrapped around her throat.

Rob was waiting at the hospital entrance, his cheeks flushed, eyes red. Dread filled his features as he saw me through the crowd in the lobby. Oh fuck. The look in his eyes was haunting. I'd only seen him look this bad once before. His arms were around me before I knew it, his hands cupped the back of my head, pressing my forehead to his. He sniffed, hanging onto me.

Fuck.

I grasped the back of his neck, accepting his strength and support. I could see the tears he was trying to hide, feel his helplessness as we stood locked in the strange embrace, each drawing strength from the other. "Tell me," I croaked. His hand slid to my shoulder as he guided me towards the ward.

"It looks worse than it is." I wasn't sure by his tone if he was telling the truth. He'd switched into doctor mode, adopted the detached voice I had come to recognise whenever he gave bad news. "There was an injury to her upper airway, so I had to intubate and she's on a ventilator. She was stabilised and moved to ICU. Given her history, they pulled the medical records. It's a good job Andy checks out because I did a little digging and Miranda has a DNR and a very specific advance directive," he whispered. I heard what he wasn't saying. If she'd have been admitted as Miranda, they would have let her die. "They are keeping her on mechanic ventilation it's the only way she's getting enough oxygen. CT showed a bronchopleural fistula, but they're confident that ventilation will give it time to heal, so they're keeping her paralysed and sedated and her blood pressure's being maintained by vasopressors. The baby has a viable heartbeat and shows no signs of distress, but they're keeping her hooked up to machines to monitor both hers and the baby's heart."

"In English," I rasped. I think I, maybe, understood two or three of the words that had tumbled from his mouth.

"She's hooked up to a lot of machines and is sleeping." He grabbed my arm as we reached the ICU. "Jesse, just prepare yourself, okay?" He sighed. Closing his eyes for a moment as if to centre himself. With a deep breath, he opened the door.

I followed him in a daze as he led me into one of the private rooms. It took me a second to realise we were even in the right place. I'd almost muttered an apology, turned, and left. She looked so small and frail, lost amongst a tangle of wires and machinery. A clear tube hung from her mouth, her chest rising and falling with the rhythmic hiss of one of the many machines by the bed. I watched lines and numbers change on things I didn't understand. I wondered if they were good, or if I was staring at a warning I couldn't decode.

This couldn't be Grace. There had to be a mistake. I stepped forward, saw the brown hair, the beautiful contours of her face. She looked so pale, so fragile. Machines and wires surrounded her, disappearing beneath thin blue blankets.

Pain speared my chest, crushing my heart.

Agony.

I couldn't breathe. I felt like I needed to run, like I needed to be anywhere but here, looking at anything but this. I needed to go home. If I went home, I'd open the door and find her there, in the kitchen, smiling, complaining about those awful drinks. This wasn't her. It was a mistake. It didn't even look like her.

No. This was a stranger. They'd got it wrong. She just looked a little like my Grace. But there was no fire there, no soul. It was a mistake.

Grace's hair never looked so limp and dull; her face had more colour.

She was at home, waiting for me.

But as much as my mind wanted to lie,

to not accept what I saw, my heart knew the truth. With each agonising beat, it called out to the shell of a woman before me. The frail, vulnerable woman. I sniffed, wiping my nose across my sleeve.

I don't know how long I'd stood there, just staring, but it must have been too long, because Rob took my arm just as my knees began to buckle, guiding me towards the only seat in a room crowded by machines. It was only as I got closer, I saw the bruise. Her entire throat was purple and mottled. I could see the place the bastard's thumb and fingers had pressed as he attempted to steal the life of the woman I loved.

Pain and anger coursed through me like a molten force burning from the very centre of my core. How could anyone do this to another person?

"He's dead?" I growl at Rob, my gaze still fixed on her. I needed assurances, assurances the bastard who put her here no longer drew breath, because if there was even the slightest possibility he was alive, if he'd been hurt and still lived, it was something I'd quickly remedy. Rob glanced away, not meeting my gaze. "Tell me the fucker's dead."

I sank into the chair, taking her hand in mine. It was warm but, at the same time, there was no warmth. Whenever I'd taken her hand in mine before, there'd always been this charge, this energy like it was more than the meeting of flesh, but of souls, like everything we were reached out to touch each other. But that energy was gone. Even her skin felt different. "How the fuck did this happen?" I squeezed her hand gently, hoping for a response, a twitch, something.

"As far as we can gather, he walked in, shot Bastian in the kitchen and then went up to her. Liv was coming over for lunch when she heard the struggle. She grabbed his gun and shot him." My stomach churned, countless possibilities playing in my mind as I considered what would have happened if not for Bastian's friend turning up when she did. I knew a little about Liv, military background now working in training people in close personal security, but that didn't change the fact she wasn't allowed to carry a weapon.

Only specially trained officers of the London Metropolitan police service could carry guns. Our laws on gun control were some of the strictest, but it didn't stop the bad guys from playing dirty. Hell, Liv wasn't even allowed to carry a taser, baton, or even pepper spray. It made me wonder why people would risk their lives against such odds. No wonder they needed elite training schools; they needed every advantage they could get.

I lifted Grace's limp hand to my lips, brushing a kiss across her knuckles before pressing it against my forehead. I'd told her I'd protect her, that I'd keep her safe. I'd failed.

## CHAPTER NINETEEN

Miranda

Two weeks later.

Voices. That's what I heard first. Words merging over one another in a string I felt should have made some kind of sense. But it didn't. I listened to the soft, low sound, straining my ears. It was something above a whisper, but not quite loud enough to be called talking.

No. Not voices, a single speaker, talking in a slow, steady rhythm. My ears felt as though they'd be stuffed with cotton wool, filled with a strange pressure as if they needed to pop and clear.

A memory of choking surfaced, of pain in my throat as people hurried around me, their forms distorted by too-bright lights as I fought to breathe, feeling like I needed to take another breath, but one not coming until air was forced into my lungs. It felt like every breath was a slow suffocation, not quick enough, not enough air.

I sucked in lungful of air. Whatever had been present before, controlling when I could and couldn't breathe, was gone. The memory returned into the fog as I realised it was Fate's voice that spoke softly, though I couldn't understand what he was saying. I felt pressure on my hand, I fought to squeeze back. Why wasn't my body doing what I wanted it to? I fought until, finally, I felt the jerky twitch of my finger. All that effort, just for it to twitch.

Another hand clamped over mine, words fell silent, and my ears finally popped.

"You're okay, everything's okay," Fate's voice soothed. I felt the pain radiating from my throat, the restriction and pressure as I tried to swallow. Why couldn't I move? Why did I hurt so much? The sensations I'd somehow ignored through the confusion, crashed over me like a tsunami, its currents dragging me under. The calmness replaced by waves of fear and pain. My lungs burned, throat screamed as my chest heaved, each struggle only making me hurt more.

Where the hell was I? Why couldn't I move?

"Grace, it's okay. Just relax. Breathe slowly. In and out," I couldn't obey, I was fighting for every breath, and the more I fought, the harder it was becoming. I could hear the rattle, the rasp of my burning chest. "Grace. I need you to listen to my voice, breathe in ..." Fate inhaled slowly, and because my body and mind knew I would follow this man into the deepest recesses of Hell, walk fire and glass to stay in his steps, I obeyed by instinct, following his lead. He spoke calmly, echoing each action as if he'd done this a thousand times before.

I wondered if he had.

"That's my girl."

My girl, my heart did a little happy dance. At least I hope it was a happy dance and not some weird kind of life-threatening palpitation. I felt my hand clamp around his, tighter now. Feeling returning to my shivering limbs. Why was I shaking?

"Where—" Was that my voice? What was wrong with my voice? It sounded gravelly, like a zombie recently risen from the dead, which wasn't too far from how I was feeling.

"You're in the hospital. You're okay," he soothed.

Hospital? My eyes slowly obeyed my command to open. I needed to see him, read his expression. Bright light stung my eyes. I didn't trust my head to move, wasn't sure I could even turn it since my neck felt as though it was trapped in a vice. Ocean blue eyes ringed by dark circles and worry looked back at me, softening as he realised I was looking. He lifted my hand, brushing his lips against my knuckles.

"You don't know how much I needed

to see those beautiful clover eyes of yours." I wanted to let my gaze explore the room, but I didn't want to break the tether between us. Besides, whenever Fate was near me, everything else just faded into grey. He was all the vibrancy, all the colour, my mind could handle. Why would I look anywhere else when I could stare at him? But I needed to know what happened.

I knew I was safe because he was here. But I didn't know anything else.

"What—" Oh. My. God. It hurt so much to talk. It felt like razor blades had gained purchase in my throat, embedding themselves deeply, vibrating with every movement. Why couldn't I remember how I got here? The last thing I remember was falling asleep in Fate's arms. My hand shot to my stomach. Was it the baby? Was something wrong?

"Everything's okay. Avery shot Bastian and attacked you." My heart stuttered, lips parting to ask the next question, but Fate was already answering. "He's okay." Fate kept his gaze on mine, answering the questions I hadn't tried to put to voice yet.

"He had to go into surgery, but there weren't any complications, he's awake and scaring the nurses." I felt a flood of relief. Bastian was as soft as snow around those he let into his life, loyal, protective, easy-going. Anyone outside however saw a different man altogether. John did that to him. Made it necessary for him to develop that hard outer shell of attitude.

John.

The words finally registered.

John had been in our home. Where was he now, how had I come to be here, if he'd been there?

"Liv shot him." Wow, he really could read my mind. "It's over."

I felt the warmth of tears trickle from my eyes, only to be wiped away by Fate's warm fingers. My heart hurt in a way it had no right to on hearing he was dead. John was a bastard, an abusive manipulating bastard. I hated him with everything I was. I hated everything about him. So why was I shedding tears over him? It was relief, I told myself. That was all. Just relief.

I lifted my hand to wipe my eye as

another silent tear escaped. I froze, studying my hand as the sparkle of something on my finger caught the light. My eyes snapped to Fate's who smiled boyishly, rubbing the back of his neck with an uneasy smile. I looked back at my grandmother's engagement ring, my thumb reaching across to stroke the warm metal resting against my skin.

He'd probably had to make up some lie so he could stay with me. I shouldn't read into this.

"I've asked you more times than I can count, in so many ways I can't remember them all. When we were children, I knew you were meant to be mine. I proposed in Grifters' Grove, at the rock pools, in the ocean as we fled the Dread Pirate Rob. I've asked you every time you've woken to see the ring. So, I'm not asking you again, Grace, because you're already mine. And if I have to wait for you to sleep to slip a ring on your finger, trick you into accepting me while you're barely coherent, that's what I'll do, a thousand times over, because a life without you next to me is no life at all. So,

I'm not asking you to marry me, I'm telling you you're already mine, just as I'm already yours. I'll spend every day, for the rest of my life, showing you the kind of love you've always deserved. Grow old with me, Grace, let me love you the way only I can. Let me be your first and last great love. Let me be your forever."

Even if I could have spoken, I don't think the words would have come. Instead, I nodded, a goofy grin on my face to match his charming smile.

## CHAPTER TWENTY

### Miranda

It had been a week since I woke in hospital. My throat still hurt like hell, but I was hardly going to complain. I was home, and that was all that mattered. Jenny had stopped by to tell me it was over, that Andy Evans could disappear back into the ether and Miranda Grace Avery could return.

Avery.

I hated that I still had his name.

I glanced at the ring on my finger. Well, I would be changing that soon enough. I don't remember much about my time in the hospital, or the events leading up to me being there. But I didn't care. I wouldn't let the past haunt me, not when I had such a wonderful future stretching before me.

I touched the thin gold band of Gran's ring. She used to spin it on her finger all the time, an idle habit. Now I understood the meaning of the smile that would curl her lips whenever she did because I wore the same one. Most people would think it was old-fashioned looking, but not me, to me it was perfection. It wasn't fancy; the band was thin from wear, not by design, and the two small diamonds were almost invisible against the pattern of the rectangular, silver setting.

I'd been convinced she'd been buried with it, or that my parents had sold it on with everything else they'd been left in the will. Turned out, after Gramps had died, she'd given her rings to Mrs Fateson for safekeeping, as if she'd known she wouldn't be able to hold on to life without Gramps beside her.

I rocked on the rocking chair in the bay window, staring at the ring in thought. I think finding out I intended to reclaim my name had come as something of a surprise to everyone. It was hard to get them to understand why I would want that monster's name back, but the truth was, it wasn't his name I wanted. It was mine.

Miranda Grace was a survivor.

When I first came back here, I'd been happy to leave the old me behind. It was only when I awoke in hospital, I realised how strong she actually was. The me I hated, had endured and suffered, but she'd also come through the other side. By trying to forget who I was, I'd been doing myself a disservice.

I heard the front door open and smiled.

"I've brought pie!" Phoebe entered with Liv in tow, wiggling the boxes in her grasp while Liv brandished two bottles of flavoured, sparkling water. I eyed the boxes hungrily. Eating solid food was still painful, but with soft fillings and delicious pastry, it was worth the pain of every mouthful.

## SAVING GRACE

"Did someone say pie?" Bastian poked his head around the kitchen door, I didn't miss the way his playful antic made him wince. He was putting on a brave show, but I'd seen the way he'd press his hand against his stomach when he coughed. Thank God John had never learnt to shoot. He had men like Jeeves for his dirty work.

Although he smiled as he greeted the new arrivals, the way he chewed the inside of his cheek as he held the phone pressed to his ear made me think something was wrong. He'd been acting strange all morning, on his phone more often than normal. But he wouldn't tell me anything. He kept saying it was business, but I didn't hear him speak to anyone.

"There better be enough for four." He hung up the phone with a guarded sigh. Sliding it back into his pocket. Something wasn't right there. His eyes flashed cold, murderous even. He blinked, his face transforming into an easy going mask of fun. I saw it for what it was. I had donned such masks for years. I wish he'd just talk to me. Let me know what was happening.

Maybe I could help.

"You mean six," Rob announced from the back where he and Fate were working to restore something Gramps had left in his shed. They were being very hush-hush about it but given the swearing and expletives I heard from the back, it wasn't going well.

"Seven, I get double." I hated my voice was still sounding a little gravelly, but Rob assured me I was healing well and in a few more weeks would feel as good as new. I dropped my hand as I found it subconsciously rubbing my throat. "Bastian." I gave Fate a nod, and he grabbed an envelope from the bookcase before joining the others in the kitchen, allowing us a moment of privacy.

I tried to clear my throat, succeeding in only making it feel rawer. "John's life insurance paid out." His other assets had been frozen because there was no way of knowing what was ill-gotten. I had assured them every penny he had was crooked, everything, except the insurance I was entitled to as his widow. I'd paid for that on the wage I earned through him.

I'm not sure if I should have been allowed it, not really. The NCA had suppressed the divorce papers, expecting me to testify against John, but now he was dead they had other plans for me. News of arrests were sweeping the nation as John's accounts hit the legal system. It was quiet at first. Precise, precision moves to isolate and remove the corrupt forces before anyone got wind of what was going to happen.

I don't know how many of their targets they rounded up. Only that the NCA and ROCU had become media heroes for cleaning up the streets. With solid evidence leading to convictions.

I think they let the life insurance money through as a way of thanks. But maybe I was overthinking. Bastian stared at the envelope in his hand questioningly, almost as if he believed by staring at it long enough the contents would make themselves known. "You have to open it," I prompted.

His eyes widened as he glanced inside

at the cheque. Bastian had lost everything when John's assets were frozen. Although the garage was in his name, and I ensured he couldn't be implicated in anything going on under that roof, the business had still been tied up in the ongoing investigations. Shut down. I didn't know if he would ever get it back, and I knew he'd worked damn hard there.

"I hear it's hard to find a good garage around here. We thought maybe you'd want to stick around." I let my eyes slide over his shoulder towards the kitchen. Liv and Phoebe were busy dishing up the pies, while Rob and Fate were seeing who could hold the most squirty cream in their mouth or something. Actually, I don't know what they were doing, but I knew long before Fate began constructing a whipped cream beard and moustache on Rob's grinning face it was only going to end one way.

He frowned at the envelope, his face contorted. "Andy, I can't—"

"You can and will." I held my hand up to cough weakly, a strange grunting noise leaving my throat as I held back further coughs. "John owes you a fresh start after everything he did. And you must know Major Donnelly's house has been put up for rent. He's gone to live with his daughter in the city."

"I don't want his money."

I placed my hand on his, stilling it before it did something foolish like rip up the cheque. Then again, if he did I would just write another one, and another, until he saw sense. "It's not his money. I took out the policy four years ago. Every payment came from me, from the wage they paid me as an accountant. John may have been wealthy, but if anything happened to me, or him, I wanted to know our children could get a clean break away from blood money." There was a long silence, and I could see how conflicted, how torn, he was.

"It's still blood money, you bled for it," he whispered, brushing his knuckles softly against my face. His touch lingered for a moment, and I knew he was thinking about all the times he had helped treat my wounds. The times when he'd heard me scream until I fell silent, knowing he couldn't risk coming to my aid before John left. But all that was in the past. Yes, I was haunted by the things that monster had done, but being here, being with Fate, had healed me.

"Think of Jake and Rosie. It's not a fortune, but it's enough for a fresh start. A new garage, a home, a family." I heard a squeal from the kitchen as Rob dove on Phoebe, giving her a cream covered Eskimo kiss as Fate, decked out like Santa, headed our way.

"My boss is always saying you can't get a good mechanic here for love nor money. If you start up, and you're as good as Grace says you are, then you'll have your first contract right off the bat." It probably would have been much more convincing if not for the cream beard. He moved to kiss me, my hand intercepting his forehead, pushing him away.

Breaking free, Fate leaned towards me.

"Don't even," I warned. Placing my fingers against his forehead, pushing him away again before he could get any closer. "Grown-ups are talking. Now, go get me food." Fate sighed, dropping his head dramatically as he moved to walk away. I was too slow seeing the way he tensed, too late reacting to the pivot. He buried his face in my neck with a growl as I shrieked, before dissolving into a fit of coughs. I watched his amusement drain, replaced by concern. So much concern, he didn't notice I'd scooped the residue from me until I rubbed it in his face. "Food. Now," I scolded trying to ignore the sticky patch of melting cream that trickled over my shoulder as I turned back to Bastian, who was watching me with something close to wonder. "Sorry, they've always been like this."

"I've said it before, but this place is good for you, Andy. You're happy."

"I'd be happier if you'd accept my gift." I steered the conversation back to where I wanted it.

"Don't you need this for the baby?"

"You know what? I have everything I need right here." I looked towards the kitchen, where Liv had armed herself. Why the hell did I have so much spray cream in this house? I hope they knew there wasn't a chance in hell I was going to be cleaning any of that up. Rob let out a yelp as Phoebe grabbed his trousers, thrusting the can inside and depressing the button.

"Are you sure you want me sticking around?"

Rob fled from the kitchen, walking awkwardly. "You're hardly going to be the winner of the best uncle competition if you don't stay to compete. I mean, I'm going to destroy you anyway, but if you're here, you'll at least think you have a chance."

"Oh, it's on," Bastian announced, his eyes lingering on Liv's for a moment. I saw how she froze in his gaze and couldn't help but smile.

Pocketing the cheque, Bastian vanished into the kitchen, grabbing the mop from behind the door. When the hell had I got so lucky? I may not have had the best life, but everything had led to this moment, and knowing that now, I knew there was not a thing I would have changed.

They say suffering tempers the greatest

souls, that we must choose to be tempered by the flame rather than consumed by it. Fate and I had been broken, burned by our past, but together we quenched each other, becoming something better, stronger.

Maybe we were never really broken to begin with, perhaps we were just two halves of a whole, waiting for the other to complete their soul and replace their missing pieces. Because I knew one thing for certain, I had never felt more alive, more loved, than I did whenever I was near him, and I would never let anything come between us again. He was mine, and I was his. Forever.

SAVING GRACE

## *A note from Emily:*

Thanks for reading Saving Grace, the final book in the Broken Fate series.

Wow, I really enjoyed writing Andy and Fate's story. I'm actually sad it's over, but worry not, you'll see more of them in Bastian, Phoebe, and Rob's stories.

I am grateful you've taken the time to read my work. If you have the chance, please leave a quick review to let others know what you thought about the book.

EMILY STORMBROOK

*Thanks for reading*

*Emily Stormbrook*

You can now follow me on Facebook and Twitter:

https://www.facebook.com/SteamyStormbrook
https://www.twitter.com/EmilyStormbrook

SAVING GRACE

## *Need another fix?*

If you're looking for something a little darker, why not take a peek at

Breaking Sin - Addicted to Sin Book one.
https://mybook.to/breakingsin

Ivy Sinclair knew the job offer was too good to be true. But she was desperate. She'd lost her father, her job, her apartment, and her best friend all in one foul swoop. She'd no choice but to hope this was a turning point.
She thought things couldn't get any worse. How wrong she had been.
Abducted and thrust into a world of violence, trapped alone with a captor who had been stalking her for years, Ivy must find a way to survive his darkness without losing herself completely as he forces her to become his, in body, mind, and soul.
He has wanted her for years, planned each move to perfection, and now all that remained was for him to break her. He wanted an heir. He wanted to hear her screams. He wanted her.

Note: This book contains graphic, non-consensual sex, abuse, and violence. If you don't enjoy reading a book containing these dark themes this book is not for you. Not suitable for under 18s.

EMILY STORMBROOK

## *Next in Series*

The next Barrett's Bay romance will be Riled Up, Bastian's story.

## *Acknowledgements*

I just wanted to say a quick thank you to my editor DJ, along with Jennifer Dean, Nancy Johnston, and Dayse, for being amazing beta readers and helping me to iron out the kinks.

I also want to thank you, the reader, for your support, and all those who have encouraged me.

Thank you x

Printed in Great Britain
by Amazon

83031806R00190